"Oh but what if I fall?"

"Oh but my darling, what if you fly?"

My dear darling granddaughters, fly high...xxx

Chapters:

Chapter 1. Ebony.

Chapter 2. Mrs Wonders. Tinkers Bell. The Little Shop of Mrs Wonders.

Chapter 3. The Party.

Chapter 4. Ebony Makes A Big Orange Wish.

Chapter 5. Wish Granted.

Chapter 6. Marmalade Meets Daddy And Orders Breakfast.

Chapter 7. Marmalade Is Granted Confidence.

Chapter 8. The Slide.

Chapter 9. NibblersFirstTeggy Plant. The Biting Plant.

Chapter 10. Mr Wormchuck Makes An Unexpected Visit.

Chapter 11. Ebony We Are All Fairies.

Chapter 12. A Sunny Day.

Chapter 13. The Paddling Pool.

Chapter 14. Neptune.

Chapter 15. The Steal.

Chapter 16. Fight For Ebony.

Chapter 17. The Day after. The Day Before The Party.

Chapter 18. The Party.

EBONY MAKES A BIG ORANGE WISH

Chapter 1

Ebony.

Let me introduce you to Ebony. Ebony is a little girl, as in not very big, she is a popular and happy girl, loved by everyone, she has curly golden hair and the biggest bluest eyes. Ebony has many friends, although some of which she hasn't met.

Ebony often says things that sometimes you can't understand, not because Ebony mumbles, more because it sounds like the wind whispering or raindrops pattering. People not wishing to appear rude tend to nod and agree, although there has never been any confusion caused by this.

It was a hot summers day two days before Ebony's 6th birthday. Mummy and Ebony were talking as they began to make Ebony's birthday cake, they were mixing ingredients together adding flour and using the eggs they had collected from the fluffy little hens who lived in their very unusual back garden.

"Mummy, when are we going to make the cat cake orange?" "I think the time is just about right Ebony, go on, go fetch it." Mummy replied. Ebony skipped to the drawer where they kept their special things, where they had placed the special cat cake colouring. Ebony had walked past the drawer many times since placing the colouring in, she was always sure she heard purring but would shake her head, dismiss it and carry on with whatever she was doing.

Chapter 2

Mrs Wonders. Tinkers Bell. The Little Shop Of Mrs Wonders.

Mummy and Ebony always loved to visit Tinkers Bell which seemed to be precisely in the middle of nowhere. No matter what it was you were wanting or needing Tinkers Bell would always have it. Mummy and Ebony loved looking around. The shop changed every day. Mrs Wonders always claimed it was never herself who moved the things around although she would giggle at some kind of private joke.

Mrs Wonders was Ebony's Grandmother which always made visiting even more special.

"Have a look around my dears," chirped Mrs Wonders, I will make us all a lovely hot pot of tea. Ebony and Mummy were busy moving things around, looking into pots and boxes, baskets and drawers, once or twice they both suspected they had heard something rattle inside a completely empty pot. They never questioned this.

Tea was brought out, steaming hot, smelling delicious and nothing like tea, a plate of the most delicious looking cakes and biscuits laid out on a very pretty and special plate having being "baked especially for your visit this morning dears." (Although how she knew about their visit was a mystery.) Jam oozed and chocolate dripped from the biggest cakes you dream of. Tarts full of strawberries and shiny blackcurrants both fresh and inviting. Biscuits full to the brim of custard filling, others drizzled over with chocolates. The tray of treats looked amazing, making Mummy and Ebony feel very hungry. They both knew if it looked amazing, because Mrs Wonders had baked them they would be amazing and completely delicious.

"Well Mrs Wonders," this is how Mummy always addressed her Mother. Not out of being polite, but because everyone called Mrs Wonders by this name. It seemed to be her first name and her last name, it seemed perfectly fitting for this wonderfully eccentric old lady. "I'm sure you know what we are here for?" Mrs Wonders nodded and smiled, "indeed I do. My darling Ebony, you go and have a look for whatever it is you need."

Mrs Wonders began pouring tea, cinnamon scents rose into the air surrounding Mummy, stroking her as a beautiful silky scarf would, she found she was completely relaxed, she hadn't realised she was tired and let out a rather large sleepy yawn.

Ebony was busy singing to herself, "psttt! I'm over here!" Ebony looked up, "that's right, I'm right over here, you can't miss me!" Ebony frowned. "Stop frowning, that's most unbecoming don't you know?" Ebony frowned more. "If the wind blows, your face will stick like that, now do stop frowning as we don't want that do we?" Ebony shook her head, "no - at least I don't think we do? Who are you and where are you?" Ebony looked around and could see nothing that would or could be having a conversation with her. "Strangest things in here." Ebony whispered.

Turning back to Mummy and Mrs Wonders, Ebony noticed a cat shaped cake tin, he was waving his paw at her. "Hello Ebony, may I say just how lovely you are when you aren't frowning. Pick me up, you'll be needing me and you also need some extraordinary orange cat cake colouring, because that is what I am. EXTRAORDINARY! Even if I say so myself, which I am doing so it would seem. Now let's find this colouring, I expect it's hiding, ready to make you jump, these extraordinary colours can be very tricky."

Cat cake tin and Ebony searched the shop, the extraordinary cat colour was indeed hiding. Every so often they heard "cold, warmer, warmer still, frozen." It blew a raspberry - it was being mischievous and playing tricks. Ebony had forgotten her shyness towards cat cake tin, they were talking in whispers to one another, trying to catch the extraordinary orange cat colouring, it however, always seemed one step ahead. "Nah, nah, nah, nah, nah nah! you can't catch me you're a big fat flea!" BANGGG! Mrs Wonders had slapped her hand down on the counter and was now holding the bottle of extraordinary orange cat cake colour. "That is very rude young man and we do not behave like that do we? Now please say you are sorry."

Ebony thought she had seen it all, a bottle of cake colouring being told off. "Sorry Ebony." The extraordinary cat cake colouring mumbled, "but I am special," he giggled.

Mrs Wonders handed Mummy the extraordinary orange cat cake colour for safe keeping and handed Ebony a cup of tea, it tasted like the creamiest, silkiest, smoothest and loveliest hot chocolate she had ever had. When she thought no one was looking, Ebony tipped some of her hot chocolate into cat cake tin, "mmm – delicious! fish soup! Thank you Ebony." Ebony smiled, odd things happened all the time in her life and had done for as long as she could remember.

It was soon time for Mummy and Ebony to return home. Mrs Wonders having carefully wrapped cat cake tin in sparkly paper could now be heard snoring. Mummy safely stored the suddenly silent extraordinary cat cake colour in her pocket. They invited Mrs Wonders to Ebony's party for a slice of what was going to be an incredible cake. Mrs Wonders smiled, "thank you, that will be perfectly charming." Mrs Wonders handed Mummy a beautiful gold box tied with green ribbon, a small selection of cakes and tarts for Daddy, she didn't want him to feel left out.

Ebony was adding the extraordinary orange cat colour slowly and carefully, squeezing the drops out as Mrs Wonders had advised them, one drop for every year. Ebony had looked at the label on the bottle and noticed in tiny writing, includes extra special surprises. As it was Ebony was hearing small meow's and purring as she stirred gently, really not at all surprised carried on stirring very much admiring the colour, "well, if nothing else, it certainly does make the cake mixture very orangey." The mixture looked so inviting Ebony wanted to taste it, checking Mummy wasn't watching, preparing to dip her finger in, "STOP THAT," cat cake mix shouted at her, "you can't eat me, I'm not baked yet and I really don't want your grubby fingers making me all germy, yuck, yuck, yuck, absolutely not, no!"

"THHHHWWWWPPPPPPPPPP," cat cake blew a long raspberry at Ebony who was looking at cat cake mix, she stood for the longest time staring, she wasn't sure if she was daydreaming. Mummy walked up behind her and placed an arm around her shoulders, it made Ebony jump. "You alright sweetheart?" "Yes it's just cat cake mix….it…it…never mind…Mummy."

Mummy and Ebony stood together holding the wooden spoon as they made a wish. Cat cake mix was now ready to be baked, they placed it in Cheerypops the oven and smiled, they knew their cake would turn out purrrfectly perfect. "BON VOYAGE, wish me luck, I don't want to look like a pig in muck," sang Cheerypops. "I think it's time to clear up," said Mummy pulling Ebony's attention away from the mischievous happenings.

Cheerypops the oven was a happy and proud oven, nothing was too much trouble, if you stood quietly you could hear him singing as he baked away, this is how Cheerypops earned his name. No matter what, Cheerypops would always bake things to absolute perfection he took pride and joy in turning out the most beautiful food. What a wonderful oven to own. Cheerypops had once belonged to Mrs Wonders. That explained everything and also nothing.

Mummy decided it was time to make the icing for cat cake, drop, drop, drop, drip, drip, drip. 6 dripdrops just as Mrs Wonders had advised, for a very special extraordinary orange cat colour. Mummy had also noticed the tiny print exclaiming - extra special surprises.

You simply never doubted Mrs Wonders, it was never a good thing to do, there would always be some kind of un-expected surprise if you did and some times not quite so nice surprises.

A young boy named Jack soon found out what happened when you doubted Mrs Wonders word. He was loudly doubting his stick of Freshlyfruity rock tasted anything like fresh fruit. He quickly unwrapped his treat and started slurping and chomping down on the rock, flavours flooded his mouth he was overjoyed, it did taste of fruit, lemony lemon slipped down his throat, red raspberries made him smile "CORRR, this aint half good!" he exclaimed to Mrs Wonders. Jack's Mother was stood as still as a statue watching her son's face change from yellow to red to blue to orange matching a colour in perfect time with the flavours he ate. Mrs Wonders simply clicked her fingers and smiled at Jack. The colour changing stopped. Jack was sad, he had thought his face changing colour was actually a really neat trick and in all fairness, it was.

Mrs Wonders was an extraordinary lady, with a head of wriggling bright gold and green hair that tended to fizz, purr, meow and bark. Sometimes you would see a puppy dog tail pop out or sometimes two green almond shaped cats eyes would be staring at you. Mrs Wonders was a lady who was always full of surprises. A lady who always had a smile and time for a chat. Mrs Wonders would bring out a pot of tea, which tasted delightful and never just like tea. People would try to decide what the wonderful flavours were in the tea but no one had managed to work it out, trying to locate a memory of this taste and becoming lost deep in thought. Mrs Wonders would bring out lovely hot gingery biscuits "freshly baked this morning."

Mrs Wonders had made some bright green jelly sweets to use for cake cats eyes and had also given Ebony some liquorice for his whiskers, having insisted that both Mummy and Ebony taste them to make sure they tasted just right, reassuring both Mummy and Ebony she could alter the taste of them quite easily, however Ebony declared they were delicious as they were, toffee apple flavour, Ebony's all time favourite. Ebony still wasn't sure what colour cake cat whiskers should be, although she knew that whatever the colour, the whiskers had to be very long and very soft. Mrs Wonders knew the liquorice whiskers would be exactly the right colour when placed on cat cake, although even she wasn't sure what that colour would be.

Let me introduce you to Ebony's Daddy. Ebony calls him Daddy because that's what he is. Daddy works long hours, no matter how tired he is when he walks through the door at night nothing could please him more than his two girls greeting him. They made a lovely family. Arthur thought his wife Lilac was a

Mummy that liked to stay home looking after their little girl, which was true, he had no clue what Lilac really was or what she could do, nor of the jokes and tricks that both herself and Ebony would play on him, not yet he didn't.

Chapter 3

The Party.

Ebony had invited all of her classmates to her party. They were gathered around watching as Ebony slowly and shakily climbed the ladder of her new slide, preparing to take her very first slide down. Ebony did not like heights. Ebony did not like heights what so ever. Feeling very unsure of herself began to wobble as she tried to sit down, the wobble wobbled worse, wobbled some more and down Ebony fell with a huge BANG. Poor little Ebony burst into tears, her knees were grazed and she had knocked out her 2 front teeth. Her friends ran to her, "sorry Ebony could happen to anyone" "cool" and in one case "CORRR, can I have a go?" One boy in particular wanted to have a go at jumping from the top of the slide to knock his front teeth out now he'd seen how exciting it was. Mummy stepped in to calm things down, cuddling Ebony she quietly slipped her hand into a pocket and gently blew fairy dust over Ebony and her friends. A flash of beautiful and shimmering colour fading in the blink of an eye.

Ebony had lost her two front teeth in the fall and having been knocked out so rudely her teeth had decided to bury themselves into the grass. They were not going to be bashed around like that thank you very much! I bet you didn't know teeth could be huffy now did you? Beautiful and shiny when good, but downright stroppy and rotten when bad. 'Nope Sir. No Siree!' they were going to bury themselves in the grass and that was all there was to it. Ebony was not going to get anything from The Tooth Fairy either, they would make sure of it. They had been planning a magnificent Falling Out Ceremony for months, with singing and dancing, guest speakers and photographers. They were to invite news reporters and had asked their very favourite Mrs Wonders to bake them a magnificent celebratory cake especially for the occasion, now they had been so rudely knocked out they would have to cancel the ceremony. They were that cross they were going to make sure tooth fairy was forced to stay away. There would be no reasoning with them.

Mummy decided the best thing to do was to make a game of hunting for Ebony's teeth, whoever found them would have a surprise to take home. Ebony's friends got onto their hands and knees and searched the garden. Harry found a worm, "Aunty Lilac I've found my worm, I lost him last week, can I take him home now please?" "No Harry, I think the best thing to do is to go and place him by the roses and let him rest for now," replied Lilac.

Searching the garden inch by inch, Ebony's teeth did not turn up. The teeth had set themselves under the grass and were still very angry. If you listened carefully you could hear them stomping around kicking things. All was not well.

Mummy called the children to her. They gathered around the table where a huge orange cat cake sat. Six sparkly candles were ready to be lit. Everyone admired this wonderful cat cake, some of them claimed the cat had winked at them, others said they heard it purring. Honestly cakes do not purr or wink – only this one did!

Mummy told them to keep watching as sometimes these cakes were tricky and would do all sorts of things you didn't expect. Mrs Wonders had once told her about a puppy cake that had got up and ran off. Mummy continued, "one day a little girl had asked for a puppy cake, puppy cake was sat on the table as good as gold until he heard the postman. The postman had come to deliver the little girl's birthday cards. Puppy cake started to bark frantically, jumped up and sprinted down the garden path after him, with every step he took a piece of cake fell away, until all that was left was a pile of cake crumbs which were barking and jumping. The poor postman stood with his head on one side deciding whether to drop the cards off or go straight home, after all, it wasn't every day a cake barked and chased you. Mummy laughed as she finished the story, the children were spellbound and wanted to hear more, they so badly wanted to see a puppy cake running and barking.

Mummy wondered if the cake had been made using extraordinary dog cake colouring with extra special surprises, she nodded in agreement with herself, it was silly of her to even doubt it, of course it had.

Mummy was looking directly at cat cake "I do hope our cat cake will not get up and run down the garden path." Giving cat cake a very hard stare continued, "waving a paw, winking an eye and purring are fine, but running off only to ruin a perfectly good cake is altogether a very bad idea indeed." Cat cake looked at Mummy giving her a very slight nod and the smallest of smiles, as if to say 'no, not me, never even thought about it,' but managing to look guilty all the same.

Ebony was standing next to cat cake, she was delighted with it, it was everything she had hoped for, if only she could have a real cat though. As the cake was lit, 6 sparkly candles fizzed, popped and whizzed around, the words 'Happy 6th Birthday Ebony' appeared like magic flying around over cat cake, who was now looking rather worriedly at the lit candles. Party poppers were jumping up from the table and popping themselves, streamers of orange were flying everywhere. Party crackers appeared in the air, pulling themselves apart with loud SNAPS, boys and girls laughing, trying to catch the many toys spilling out.

Cat cake decided to join in, after all what was the point of - with extra surprises, if all he was allowed to do was lie on a table, no this just would not do. Cat cake smiled and started blowing bubbles, everyone quickly realised the bubbles had even more gifts in them, some had tiny fairies, some toy cars, others had puppies and kittens, horses and unicorns. The orange bubbles had sweets and chocolate gifts with rainbow coloured confetti that grew into squeaking pink mice which exploded into pink shimmering sparkles which were now shooting high in to the sky. The sky turned black and a firework display began. Cats jumped and twirled, dogs sat up and begged, horses jumped imaginary fences, lions roared, hens scattered pecking around, elephants spurted water, the children watched in awe. No one had ever seen anything like this. Ever. They were happy and having a truly amazing time, they didn't know how this was happening, they didn't care how it was, but they were all delighted it was.

Later, the children watched as cat cake waved, smiled and purred, he started walking around showing off, doing tricks until Mummy looked and wagged her finger at him, "no, no, no, you aren't going anywhere, now please lay back down." He was a good cat cake and lay down although he was still smiling and waving. He whispered to Ebony "Happy Birthday, I hope we meet again very soon."

"Make a birthday wish Ebony, blow the candles out and make a wish, go on!" The girls and boys cheered her on. "I wish for a cat, I would love an orange cat, just like this cat cake." Ebony blew. They watched sadly as the candles stopped fizzing and whizzing and watched as the Happy Birthday sign disappeared.

"Fingers crossed Ebony, you never know," squeaked a tiny voice, Ebony turned quickly to where the voice had come from but all she could see was a large piece of cat cake flying with difficulty across the garden all by itself. Mummy had given Ebony's friends a large slice of cat cake and had cut some more for Mrs Wonders and extra slices 'just in case.' Ebony wondered 'who Justin Case was, had she met him?' Ebony took a bite of her cat cake, it tasted delicious, chewing and slurping the icing. Ebony was watching the piece of cat cake which was still struggling to fly across the garden, her palms felt itchy and sticky, maybe it was the icing?

Mummy decided that as all of Ebony's friends had tried to cheer her up and all had searched for a very long time for the missing teeth, that each and every one of them deserved an extra present. Somehow and no one was quite sure how, everyone received an extra party bag and in that bag was a large present which had been wrapped in pink, purple or rainbow sparkles, glittering like star drops and diamonds. All the children opened them hurriedly and whooped in delight as they found they had received their most wanted present ever. How did Mummy do it? No one really knows to be honest. Probably, even maybe it was magic from The Fairy Kingdom Above.

Ebony's friends gathered to hug her goodbye. All of them were very sad to be leaving after having had such an amazing party, their party bags were full of the gifts they had caught, sweets and chocolates, another slice of cat cake, which they were to share with their brothers and sisters. If you looked quickly at cat cake, there was definately a shimmer, quite probably fairy dust, but no one noticed.

Chapter 4

Ebony Makes A Big Orange Wish.

That night Ebony was still upset about her missing teeth. Mummy tried to make her feel better and told her "when everyone is asleep tonight, the fairies that live in our garden will come out of their homes and look for your teeth, they will leave a little present for you." Ebony smiled. Mummy hugged Ebony tight, "as this is your birthday you are allowed to make an extra special wish tonight, a wish so special all the fairies can hear it, remember to say please and thank you, it helps to bond the wish." Ebony nodded.

Mummy was always talking about fairies and always reminded her to say good night to them. Ebony huddled in closer on Mummy's lap, drinking her cup of warm milk before bed. Ebony would always say the goodnights her Mummy had taught her years ago, since before Ebony could remember when. "Goodnight fairies, keep safe in the night, keep safe in your flight."

Mummy knew exactly what Ebony would wish for tonight, something she had asked and pleaded for every night. A cat. Not just any old cat though, her cat had to be orange with long fur and even longer whiskers and the biggest greenest eyes.

Ebony had already chosen his name.

Ebony was snuggled down in bed, Mummy kissed her on her nose and pulled the duvet over her. "Remember please and thank you. Sleep well my beautiful daughter, dream of fairies and all things good." Ebony often thought she could hear butterfly wings beating together as Mummy walked out of her room.

Ebony waited until Mummy had gone downstairs, she could hear her talking on the phone, she knew she would be on it a long time, safe enough to get out of bed for a few moments, she rushed over to her cat book and found the page where there was a picture of the cat she so badly wanted, she placed the book open under her pillow, crossing her fingers Ebony began her wish.

"Please fairies, please I hope you can hear me? Mummy says you can. My Mummy is the best in the world you know. It was my birthday today and I fell from the top of my new slide. I've lost my two front teeth and that is the problem, I did loose them, everyone looked for them but no one could find them. Cora and Erin are my best friends, they thought they had found them but they were just white pebbles, not my teeth, so I can't leave them out for you. Mummy told me you secretly make them all new and sparkly again ready for another baby to grow into them, a baby like Emily maybe? I'm very sorry but mine are still in the garden I promise to look for them again tomorrow." With this she squeezed her eyes tight shut and pressed her hands together, "what I really would love please is a big fluffy orange cat with beautiful green eyes and really long soft whiskers, I hope he won't mind me hugging him."

Little did Ebony know her Mummy was the Queen Fairy of all Fairy Kingdom Above and Below and at that very moment was making a phone call to Pickle, a mischievous but lovely little fairy who lived hidden amongst the flowers and trees in their garden.

Ebony sleepily finished, "thank you fairies, good night sleep tight, safe flig…" Ebony was fast asleep.

Ebony knew her Mummy was special. All Mummies are special and they all have fairy dust to sprinkle, should it be needed. Mummy was always doing strange things, but to Ebony, they were perfectly normal. Everyone had an oven that talked, of course they did.

Mummy would always have fairy dust ready to sprinkle on any cut, bruise, bump or bang. Ebony thought once or twice she had seen something sparkle when Mummy made her feel better, especially when it was followed with a cuddle, it always made everything right.

The fairies were by now gathering around Ebony's bed, tiny little girls with beautiful wings made for them by butterflies, each fairy owned a wand made from woven golden spider webs, each wand had a pink and gold glittering star on the top, these were wishes waiting to be made. They sparkled just as brightly and as beautifully as unwished wishes could ever sparkle.

The fairies thought Ebony so beautiful, such a sweet child, they had watched as she had fallen from the slide, they wanted so badly to fly over and help but they knew they had to stay out of sight. Some of the fairies had later placed some magic around the slide making sure no one would ever fall from it again. They were very cross with the slide for being so mean and for making her fall. No one did that to their Princess, no one.

"Pickle can you pull the book out a little bit more for me, I can't see much of the picture, Ebony's teddy bear is in the way." Try as the little fairies might they could not move teddy bear, who looked rather splendid in a flowery outfit of matching hat, scarf and waistcoat. Pickle didn't think this would be a problem. We should write a message to Ebony telling her not to worry about her missing teeth, that we can always grow a few extra." In the biggest writing they could manage, which of course was very tiny to us, they wrote, Princess Ebony, Happy Birthday. Wish Granted! Ps., don't worry about your teeth, enjoy your cat and treat him well, lots of love, Pickle, Starlight, Summer and

Breezy. Pickle giggled as she added XXX at the end of the message.

The fairies knew about Ebony wanting a cat, they knew she had already chosen a name. They had listened to her prayers, her wishes and her thoughts since the day she had been born 6 years before. A day when Nature had rejoiced in her Birth. The day the sky had turned pink, blue, orange, gold and purple all at the same time, a wonderful day as Queen Fairy Lilac had given birth to a tiny daughter, a Fairy Princess.

Princess Fairy Ebony would one day be able to look after herself, but even when that day arrives she will be protected and loved by all of Fairy Kingdom Above and Below. Little did she know of the adventures and fun she would have. Adventures that were just about to begin.

"Well done Pickle and Starlight." Summer was delighted and continued, "look Ebony has drawn hearts around him, shall we put some hearts on a collar for the cat?" they asked each other? "Come on let's make a spell."

Pickle and Twinkle were standing next to each other with their wands held high, the stars on the top gleaming and shining as they began. "Hold on, let us join in" called the others, we want to help grant her this wish too."

So, with a swish that was as light as a butterfly kiss they all flew on to Ebony's squishy pillow and began their spell.

"Oh Great One, Oh Majesty, please tell. Oh Great One, Oh Majesty please do not dwell, a cat of orange, with long fluffy fur and green eyes aglow, a huggable, humble ragpuss with humour and whiskers aflow, please send him right now and complete our spell...one, two, three!"

All wands touched at the star. 'POP!!!' Brilliant flashes of golden and pink sparks flooded Ebony's bedroom as Ebony slept on completely unaware the fairies had granted her wish and on her bed now lay the softest cat of orange with the biggest greenest eyes and the longest whiskers anyone had ever seen.

Cat was not only very surprised, he was also super grumpy at being so rudely woken up. Pickle and Starlight were chatting excitedly to each other as they reached out to stroke him. "Oh look at ginger cat, isn't he lovely?" Pickle reached into his fur and tickled him.

"I am NOT a ginger cat at all, please ensure in future you keep to the facts. I am an in fact an ORANGE cat, thank you very much!" Orange cat seemed to be very particular about things but he was ORANGE and that was all there was too it. "TTTTTHHHHHHWWWRRRRRPPPP," cat blew a raspberry at Pickle and flicked his paw at her. Pickle laughed, stumbled backwards and laughed more. The kind of laugh where the more you try to stop the more you laugh. Starlight managed to catch her. "Shhh, we're going to wake Ebony," they were all laughing, Summer and Breezy too, that flick of cat's paw was just the funniest thing. Sparks were shooting out of their wands, flying around the room, goodness knows what they were doing but Fairy Mischief was definitely being made.

With a nod of his sleepy head, as if to say all is sorted and explained now cat curled up and went to sleep.

"Oops! Were we supposed to make him talk?" Pickle was giggling and Starlight had mischief in her eyes, winked and wrinkled her nose, "no, but it'll be much more fun for Ebony having a cat that can talk, let's leave him as he is."

The fairies flew off to find their friends, they had lots of baby teeth to collect, this was a very serious job indeed. Lots of Ebony's friends were also growing their big teeth and were saying good bye to their baby teeth. Every one had to be collected, not one should be missed. Lots of little gifts were to be given to all the children who had looked after their teeth well and had kept their baby teeth clean and shiny. This made the fairies very happy.

Chapter 5

Wish Granted.

Early the next morning as Ebony began to stir, she tried to move her legs, she couldn't understand why they felt squashed down, opening her eyes she blinked once, blinked twice, then three times, then rubbed her eyes, no she wasn't seeing things, there on her bed was a huge orange cat, who was fast asleep and snoring, snoring very loudly to be precise.

Ebony prodded it, convinced she was dreaming. "OUCH! That isn't nice don't you know?" Cat opened his large green glowing eyes.

"My wish came true. MY WISHHHHH CAMEEEEEE TRUEEEEE!!!!!!!!!!!" Ebony was up and dancing around. Cat looked on and yawned. "I believe you wanted an orange cat? I am the cat you wished for am I not? I do rather like my name - I bet you never expected me to speak, now did you?" Cat knew Ebony had not asked for him to speak. She stood now with her mouth open and her eyes even wider open, looking directly at cat as he spoke.

"You didn't just talk to me did you? I think I'm still asleep." Ebony whispered. Cat stood up and grabbed the hat from the teddy bear, bowed down low sweeping the hat in front of him. "MARMALADE at your service Princess Ebony." Ebony ran to Marmalade and pulled him into a hug, Marmalade smiled. He already loved Ebony.

"Mummy, MUMMMMMYY! The fairies granted my wish and now Marmalade is on my bed, come see, come see pleassssseeee!" Mummy smiled to herself, "well of course they did sweetheart it was a very special wish wasn't it?" Daddy nudged Lilac, "Is that the cat you saw in the pet shop last week?"

"Oh what a magnificent Marmalade he is," Mummy said as she slowly and gently stroked the sleeping Marmalade. His big green eyes opened slowly, blinked and smiled at Mummy. "Mummy there is something I need to tell you, it's quite important." Marmalade yawned and nodded, looking directly at her, "hello, I'm Marmalade, you already knew that though. I talk though you didn't know that did you? It beats Meow, paws down, however, it's been lovely to meet you though if you don't mind I'm going back to sleep. It's very hard work being a talking cat don't you know?" ZZZZzzzzZZZZzz. Marmalade was snoring again, very loudly again, apparently Marmalade snored loudly most of the time.

Marmalade was still snoring, Mummy laughed, turning to Ebony whispered "did you say you wanted a sleepy, snorey, talking cat?" Mummy reached out to stroke his silky soft head, he was as beautiful as beautiful could be. "Come down stairs and we can make breakfast, I think it's for the best if we don't tell people Marmalade can talk, they already think we are strange, this would be the icing on the cake so to speak." Ebony nodded. "Mummy, I'm wondering how Daddy will be, I'm sure he will think we are playing tricks on him." Ebony answered very seriously.

Chapter 6

Marmalade Meets Daddy And Orders Breakfast.

A fresh new day, helped them decide lovely fresh boiled eggs would be perfect for breakfast, they were laid by the pretty little hens that lived in their back garden, milk for Ebony and a hot fresh tea for Mummy. Chattering away to each other, sometimes in quiet whispers and other times laughing loudly, both were happy and smiling. "Later on Ebony, we need to go and buy some food for Marmalade, a cat that size is going to take quite a lot of feeding." Mummy was smiling, unsure how many tins a day would be required.

Daddy came downstairs and sat at the breakfast table. Pulling the newspaper towards him he saw the eggs. "Boiled eggs for breakfast, delicious!" He was soon eating toast and eggs and slurping hot tea. He hadn't noticed Marmalade, he hadn't noticed when he climbed into the chair besides him. Daddy finally noticed Marmalade. His face went white. "Oh, what a gorgeous cat!" Daddy became quiet, he was lost in a memory from a different time. "He's exactly like the cat I had as a young boy, he even has the same big whiskers and eyes." Reaching out to stroke Marmalade. "What a beautiful cat you are."

Marmalade smiled and offered Daddy his paw to shake. "I am Marmalade it's very nice to meet you. Is ok if I call you Daddy?" Daddy started choking, he was choking really rather well, having just taken a sip of tea the precise moment Marmalade had chosen to speak. Daddy's eyes were wide open and he was frantically shaking his head "tell me I imagined that, tell me that cat DID NOT SPEAK!" Marmalade patted Daddy's arm, "of course I did, you heard me, did you not? I speak purrrrfect English, get it? PUURRRFECT...as in cats purr?" Ebony and Mummy were laughing just as much as anyone could laugh. They were watching Daddy who was staring at this large, orange talking cat in complete shock, he couldn't believe what was happening, he was sure it was all a very strange dream. Cats do not talk, everyone knows that. They just do not talk. Marmalade does and we know that don't we? "Calm down Daddy, I'm a cat that can talk, you'll be fine once you get used to me."

"Boiled eggs, yummy, yes please," said Marmalade, "they look delicious, oh and possibly some toast with butter please, it has to be butter, the rest do not taste right, oh and could I possibly trouble you for a saucer of creamy fresh milk please?" Daddy was a funny red colour. A large orange cat was sitting at the table next to him, he talked, he had made a joke and had ordered breakfast. He pinched himself really hard, he knew this was a dream. "OUCH!" It was no dream, that pinch really hurt.

"I really can't see what is so funny," Marmalade looked at Ebony as he said this. Cats eat breakfast, of course they do. Tell me please, oh do please tell me you weren't going to feed me that mushy stuff that comes out of a tin were you?" Ebony and Mummy looked at each other, both shaking their heads really rather quickly, Marmalade looked at them suspiciously. "That stuff is rather nasty you know?" "No, no, of course not, we were wondering how many eggs you would like for breakfast was all?" Mummy said rather too quickly looking embarrassed.

Daddy was still in a state of shock pointing at Marmalade repeating "he's just ordered breakfast and called me Daddy! Say something else, this is not real, oh! I know, he's a speaking toy isn't he? Go on, say something - anything." Daddy was still very red in the face and was roughly prodding Marmalade in his tummy, he was determined to find where the batteries went. Try as he might he could not find anything other than a large furry cat belly.

"Stop prodding me it hurts. Now Daddy, why do bees hum? Come on this one is easy!" Daddy sat with his mouth wide open staring at Marmalade. Marmalade put his big fluffy paw on Daddy's hand and gently squeezed. "Now do you know why bees hum?" Daddy looked at Marmalade and shook his head. "Bees hum because they don't know the words," he slammed his paw down on the table and started laughing, "oh I'm so good, I even make myself laugh." Marmalade hadn't noticed Mummy and Ebony, their faces were also red and getting redder trying not to laugh. This lovely huge, raggedy, fluffy, funny, talking cat Marmalade had arrived.

Lilac placed a warm hand on her husbands shoulder, reaching in her pocket and as Ebony suspected, out came something sparkly, she thought it must be fairy dust, Lilac gently blew it all over him.

Standing up and clearing his throat he suddenly felt so much better. "So what if we have a talking cat, it's really not the end of the world and Marmalade is fabulous" he announced.

"Marmalade, it's lovely you tell jokes and it's fine calling me Daddy and also you can call Lilac Mummy." He reached out once again to stroke the wonderfully soft ears that were on the wonderfully soft head that was Marmalade. "One more thing, welcome to the family Marmalade!" Marmalade bowed his head and raised it again, "thank you all so very much." Lilac noticed tears welling up in Marmalades eyes, she knew then that he was a lovely caring gently catpus. Mummy had fallen head over heels in love with this very different cat, Ebony had loved him since the moment she had opened her eyes, Daddy was over the moon with him, he was indeed an incredibly special cat. Marmalade in turn loved each and every one of them, he was happy to be part of this family, he knew this was exactly where he belonged.

No matter how hard he tried Marmalade couldn't stop himself as he lapped at his saucer of milk 'purr, purr, purr,' he was enjoying it so much. Ebony reached out to stroke him, she knew you really shouldn't touch an animal when it is eating, so quickly pulled her hand back. "No, no, it's ok to stroke me anytime, I loved being stroked." Marmalade said between laps.

"I do have an itch between my shoulders though so if you don't mind, would you please scratch it for me?" Purr, Purr, Purr.

Chapter 7

Marmalade Is Granted Confidence.

Ebony and Mummy only had to look at one another and both would start to giggle. "Bagpuss, Bagpuss, you sleepy old furry catpus," Mummy whispered, "NO!" Shouted Marmalade. "Bagpuss is pink and cream and he's a teddy bear! I'm a cat! I am real, I am, I am!"

So not only did they have a cat that talked, they had a cat that was easily upset. We are going to have to be careful what we say around Marmalade, we can't have him upset over a few mistaken words. Perhaps we can ask the fairies to make another spell so he is a little bit more confident? I will ask them."

Lilac rang Pickle, telling her all about Marmalade becoming upset when she had started to whisper the Bagpuss song to him, he felt we didn't think he was a real cat. "Pickle would you please find a spell to make him a little bit more confident?" "Let me see, that shouldn't be too difficult," replied Pickle, "isn't he a smashing cat though?" Pickle started to wave her wand.

"Come here and now a little wish, for a cat with no confidence but has a big fluffy tail to swish, make him bold, make him bright, make a little of his fear take flight."

With a flick of her wand and a little 'POP!' from the star, the spell had been made. Marmalade sat upright. "ICANDOKICKBOXING!" Ker Pow! Bang! Swish!" He looked at Mummy and laughed, "Sorry I saw that on a film somewhere, Keanu…erm…someone…I can't remember," he laughed. Lilac looked on, "perhaps we should have done something about his sense of humour?" Mumbling quietly to herself.

Ebony loved Saturday mornings and wanted to play in the garden, she thought she may try looking for her missing teeth again. "Marmalade, are you coming to play in the garden?" Ebony asked. "I'll be there in a few minutes," he shouted as he ran upstairs.

Ebony really did not expect to see Marmalade walking across the garden towards her wearing a flowery summer hat, a matching scarf and definately not the waistcoat, it was the entire outfit he'd taken from the bear sitting on her book the fairies had granted the wish from. She tried not to laugh, instead she called out and told Marmalade how nice he looked.

Chapter 8

The Slide.

Marmalade flicked his paw which in cat language meant 'I do look rather splendid even if I say so myself.' Marmalade hadn't quite got the right idea about the slide, he was standing at the top, slowly and carefully he started to walk down, he looked rather pleased with himself and decided he wanted to do it again. "Look at me Ebony, I'm sliding," Marmalade called out. "I bet I am the only cat ever that can do this." Oh dear, thought Ebony, how do you tell a cat that is not how you slide? Ebony looked at his outfit again, smiled and decided on, "that's a very good slidey walk Marmalade." Ebony wondered if Marmalade somehow knew about her accident with the slide and about her teeth being knocked out?

Mummy joined them, "what are you two doing?" Mummy was looking at Marmalade, "aren't they the clothes from your teddy bear Ebony?" Ebony nodded, "he says he's trend setting and looks very fashionable, but I don't know what that means Mummy, he also thinks he is sliding down the slide too, but he's only walking down it. He is very happy though," she added suddenly.

Marmalade was now running down the slide 'WHEEEEEEEE' he called to Mummy. "Mummy see me, I'm sliding!" Mummy looked at Marmalade, a huge smile spread across her face, she smiled to him, what on earth does he look like?

Ebony noticed next to the slide a small plant had grown, she knelt down to take a close look. She really hadn't seen anything like it before. "It's a NibblersFirstTeggy Plant" called Marmalade. "I haven't seen one for ages." Ebony looked up still not sure whether it was safe to touch this plant, but prodded it all the same, nothing happened so she prodded at one of the shiny white buds. Marmalade had joined her, he flipped at it with his paw, the plant slapped him hard on the nose "OUCH," cried Marmalade. "Daddy" Ebony called out. Daddy had followed Lilac outside with his cup of tea. "Daddy, come see." Daddy knelt down and studied the plant, a strange plant with tiny white shiny buds. "What did you say it was called Marmalade?" "NibblersFirstTeggy Plant" repeated Marmalade, well that's the posh name for it, there is another name for it." Daddy decided to jab the plant with his fingertip, jabbing at the tiny white bud. "OUCH THAT PLANT BIT ME!!!" shouted Daddy loudly, looking at the tinniest bite mark on his fingertip, watching and turning very pale as the smallest ever pinprick of blood appeared. "Ah yes," Marmalade chirped in helpfully, "Biters Plant." Marmalade looked at Daddy, who always fainted at the sight of blood. Noticing how white Daddy was insisted he sat down, "you will be ok Daddy, I promise, but first perhaps sit down for a while."

"Marmalade how do you know what it is called?" Ebony asked him. "I don't know I just have a feeling that if I were to wave my paw about and say a few words I could make magic," he replied honestly. "Go on," said Ebony, "make Daddy's cup of tea keep filling itself up" she whispered to Marmalade.

"Cup of tea, drink so fine, REFILL yourself all the time!"

Marmalade waved his paw about and 'POP!' "We will have to wait and see if anything happens." The thought of Daddy looking puzzled made them both giggle. Neither of them believed for a moment that a spell had been made.

"Daddy please come and play on the slide with me." Marmalade pleaded, "drink your tea, then come on the slide with me please Daddy?" Marmalade knew about Ebony falling and knew how scared of the slide she now was, he wanted to show her it could be really good fun.

Ebony sat down next to Daddy's empty teacup and glanced into it, she was both amazed and delighted to see the tea gently refilling itself.

Daddy and Marmalade were sliding down together, Daddy on his tummy and Marmalade standing on Daddy's back waving his flowery hat to Ebony and Mummy.

Ebony and Mummy were laughing and enjoying the fun. Mummy felt this was a moment to be captured forever in time so quickly fetched her camera, she was looking around and knew Pickle fairy would be around somewhere, whenever Mummy took a photo, you could guarantee Pickle would photobomb it. It didn't matter wherever or whenever you took a photo, Pickle would be in it - somewhere. Ebony watched as

Mummy waved her finger at something hiding over in the flowers.

'BRRRINGGGG....BRRRINGGGG' the telephone sounded in the hall. "I'll grab it," said Daddy, he stood up and walked inside. A few minutes later he came back out, being a rather tidy man, went to put his cup and saucer in the kitchen, as he picked it up he noticed he hadn't drank any. He shook his head. "I'm sure I drank my tea," he said out loud, "couldn't have done!" Sitting back down on his deckchair he began to drink his tea, he was enjoying watching Ebony and Marmalade play, though he wondered why they were laughing so much. He had been very surprised to discover a plant had grown overnight, a plant that bit people really very hard a nasty, super vicious thing! He looked at the enormous plaster on his finger. Marmalade had been quite right, the bite had healed almost instantly, however Daddy would not take the plaster off, not even to have a quick look. Daddy was very scared of blood and nothing would make him look at the almost invisible mark on his finger.

Half an hour later Daddy was still sipping tea. He look puzzled as he looked at his cup. It was full. He hadn't drank any. He must have really had a bad time of being bitten so viciously. Taking a few really big mouthfuls drank it all, he was beginning to feel quite full now as he sat his cup back down next to him. He picked a daisy and started to examine it, "next thing you know this daisy will probably turn into a gigantic purple worm, the way things are!" Ebony and Marmalade smiled at each other, Marmalade waved his paw, 'POP!' Oh no, he was just playing, he hadn't meant or even wanted to make any kind of spell.

Marmalade had no idea how clever he was making fairy spells. Ebony and Marmalade noticed the grass starting to bubble up and down and wriggle around them, purple, pink and green fizzy sparkles had started shooting high into the sky. They looked at each other and were suddenly very, very quiet.

"I need some biscuits to go with this tea," Daddy said walking off to find some. Picking up his cup, tea spilt down his trousers, his face puzzled and annoyed. "What in blazes name is going on?" he asked angrily to no one in particular. His tea cup was full again. "I know I drank it, I know I did, maybe Lilac made me another cup and I didn't see her put it down?" Walking in to the kitchen he found his favourite biscuits and started dip some in his tea, something he loved to do, he felt better. "Thank you for my tea Lilac, oh and Mrs Wonders is calling in later." Lilac looked at him and shook her head, "I didn't make you any tea?"

Daddy drank his tea once again and put the cup back on the draining board, put the biscuits back in the cupboard and went to wash his cup, it was full again. "I think I need a holiday," he was very upset.

Back outside and still annoyed, Daddy noticed Ebony whispering to Marmalade. "I think we need to stop the spell making the tea refill, Daddy is upset." Marmalade nodded and began.

"Cup of tea, drink so fine STOP refilling all the time!" Marmalade waved his paw a few times 'POP!'

Chapter 9

NibblersFirstTeggy Plant. The Biting Plant.

Ebony called to Mummy, "Mummy please tell us about the Biting Plant." Lilac looked around. "Listen Ebony I do know this plant if I tell you about it you must promise not to tell anyone." Ebony nodded, agreeing. "It's the NibblersFirstTeggy Plant or as Daddy will now remember it - the Biting Plant." Mummy giggled, poor Arthur. "When little children loose their baby teeth in an accident and can not find them like you did yesterday, the teeth set themselves into the ground and grow. They wait until the Tooth Fairies find them and can pick all the freshly grown Teggy Buds, they are the things that nipped Daddy's finger. The plant is very clever and protects itself from anyone trying to pick these lovely new teeth buds, it bites very hard anyone who isn't something to do with our Fairy Kingdom but gives only a tiny little nip to those of us who are - as a gentle reminder that these are for the Tooth Fairies only and not meant to be played with.

The fairies usually collect teeth straight from the children who have outgrown their baby teeth, from under their pillows at night, after the children have fallen asleep. The fairies watch all the boys and girls and know where and when to visit. They leave a coin in exchange for a tooth as a way of saying 'thank you.' The Tooth Fairies look after the teeth and get them ready for the next baby who will need them, not a moment too soon, not a moment too late. They really are very clever. They are also our best friends.

Ebony wondered why the plant hadn't bitten her when she had jabbed her finger at it. Probably just lucky, she thought to herself smiling, she hadn't wanted her finger bitten any time soon.

Ebony questioned further "but Mummy, Marmalade knew what this plant was, how could he, how would he know about it?" A gentle hug from Mummy ended the questions.

"Sparkle," Mummy spoke quietly, "there is a NibblersFirstTeggy Plant growing in our garden by the slide, they must be Ebony's teeth, anyway would you be a poppet and remove it tonight please?" Mummy smiled. "Thank you, bye, bye."

Chapter 10

Mr Wormchuck Makes An Unexpected Visit.

Mummy looked at Marmalade was staring in horror at an enormous purple worm. The worm having spotted her, wriggled, turned and started worming his way over. "Hello Lilac how are you dear?" Worm noticed Ebony who was trying to hide behind a tree and really not doing a very good job at all. Worm wanted to say hello and introduce himself. "Hello Ebony, he smiled in greeting. "AAAAAARRRRRGGGGHHHHH!" Ebony started crying and ran to Mummy. Mummy would make it better, make it all go away, she hoped.

Worm was enormous with an amazing amount of pink and green hair growing out of his head, puddles of slime dripping from his nose.

Marmalade joined Ebony putting an arm around her trying to make her feel safe. He looked sad and upset, poor Marmalade knew he had caused this. "Marmalade what did you wish for in your spell?" Ebony asked between big wet sobs. Marmalade decided the insides of his paws needed urgent inspection, paying very close attention to his claws, he didn't want to look at Ebony not when she was crying and it being his fault. Worm was worming his way slowly over to Lilac once again. Ebony and Marmalade were hiding behind her. "I didn't mean too," sobbed Marmalade, "I'm really sorry." Mummy turned giving them a very hard we will talk later look, then turned back to worm.

Marmalade wasn't scared of worm, he was very sorry he had upset Ebony. Not quite knowing what to do and being scared of getting squashed as worm was the size of a bus, he picked up a blade of grass and tickled worms belly, it chuckled, wriggled, squiggled and finally started laughing.

'Hello Lilac, that didn't go quite as planned, I only wanted to say hello to Ebony. Sorry Lilac." As he spoke he peeked behind her and looked directly at Marmalade. "Hello Marmalade old chap, how are you? Haven't seen you for an age. Have your jokes improved? Do stop tickling me it makes me sneeze!" "MARMALADE STOP!" Mummy screamed, "that's a really bad thing, we do not want that happening, I guarantee it!" Ebony looked at Marmalade saying absolutely nothing, after all what could "she say?

"Mr Wormchuck, how lovely to see you again, bit of a problem though, we can't really have giant purple worms in our garden in daylight hours, a worm so big everyone can see it. I'm not sure how we would explain it."

It was this precise moment that Mrs Wonders walked in to the garden. Ebony watched as she walked up to worm. "Hello Mr Wormchuck, how are you and Mrs Wormchuck? Any exciting news to be told?" She gave him a slight hug trying to avoid the copious amounts of slime. So, thought Ebony, if Mummy knows him, Mrs Wonders knows him and Mr Wormchuck knows them and Marmalade, though goodness knows how, surely he wasn't a bad worm?

Unfortunately this was the very same time Daddy chose to look out the kitchen window. Seeing a gigantic purple worm with pink and green hair talking to his wife, Marmalade and Ebony and have a hug with Mrs Wonders was all just far too much, far too much in fact and the best thing he could do would be to faint, so faint he did, down he went. He was out cold before he hit the floor.

Marmalade looked at Mummy who bent and scooped him in to her arms. "It's ok Marmalade." Mummy stroked Marmalade, his fur had taken on a very red embarrassed glow to it. He is a very kind worm and means no harm to anyone. You've made a mistake and somehow you summoned Mr Wormchuck, who by the way is one of Ebony's Guardians, he only ever comes here at night. He seems to remember you, why don't you two have a chat while I sort things out?"

Silently and unseen Mummy reached into her pocket, found a pinch of fairy dust sprinkled it over Ebony and Marmalade giving them a reassuring hug.

Mr Wormchuck was talking to Mrs Wonders. They were talking about Marmalade, Mrs Wonders was explaining she had been the one to make the extraordinary orange cat cake colour with extra surprises and that sometimes even she did not know what the extra surprises would be. Mr Wormchuck was arguing loudly he had known Marmalade for almost forever. It was rapidly turning heated. Neither would agree to disagree and neither would back down, surprisingly both were right.

"Mummy, Marmalade was only pretending when he made that spell. He didn't know what he was doing, when we saw that something was happening, he tried to put it right but he didn't know what he had done so didn't know how to stop it," Ebony continued, "when he saw how scared I was of the worm, he started crying too. He's very upset Mummy and he is very sorry."

Mummy smiled. "It's probably not a good thing having daisies turning into gigantic purple worms. Where did Marmalade get such an idea from?" Ebony looked up and knew she had to tell Mummy the truth. "When that Biters Plant bit Daddy, he sat down with his cup of tea. I asked Marmalade how he knew what the plant was called, he told me he felt he could do magic. I didn't believe him so I asked him to make Daddy's cup keep filling itself up. Daddy kept finding his cup of tea was full again every time he had drank it empty, he picked up a daisy and said "that the way things were going around here, the daisy would probably turn into a giant purple worm!"

Ebony looked at Mummy, not knowing if she were cross or not. "That was not a nice thing to do to Daddy, but it wasn't terrible either." Mummy winked and smiled, "no harm done." The gigantic purple worm, Mr Wormchuck is a problem though. Mr Wormchuck loves sniffing at things, so there is every chance you will end up inside his nose. If he sneezes not only do you get blown out, you end up covered in sticky green sparkly slime, that's not the only problem though, the smell is awful and people like Daddy faint. It's best if we stop whatever it is Marmalade did.

"Mr Wormchuck." Lilac called to the gigantic worm who was laughing at one of Marmalades jokes, "Could I talk to you for a moment please?"

Marmalade decided Mr Wormchuck was a friendly worm and had started to tell him some of his wonderful jokes. Mr Wormchuck was actually a very kindly worm thought it only polite and correct to laugh, even though they weren't funny jokes. They were getting on like old friends. Actually they were old friends. Marmalade couldn't remember anything but memories were stirring from a time long ago.

"Mr Wormchuck, please," Lilac called. "Ah Lilac dear, you're back, how lovely it's been to see you all." He smiled. I suppose I should be heading back home though. Do you remember how we first met?" Nodding Lilac went a funny shade of embarrassed red, a lot like the colour of Marmalades fur Ebony noticed.

AAAAAAATTTTTTTIIIIIIISSSSSSHHHHHHHHOOOOOOOOOOOO, A-A-AAAAAAAATTTTTTTTIIIIIISSSSSHHHHHHOOOOOOO, CHOOOO, CHOOO!!!!!!!

Lilac's eyebrows raised. She had known from the very first sneeze.

"Mr Wormchuck, please lower your head a moment?" Lilac really did not want to poke around the inside of Mr

Wormchucks nose although she had no choice as she had known immediately who was caught up in all the slime.

"If I've told you a thousand times and then a thousand more it still wouldn't be nearly enough." Mummy was talking to Mr Wormchucks nostril fishing around inside the green sparkly bogey slime now covering her hand. Grabbing at something small she pulled her hand out, trying not to grimace in front of Mr Wormchuck, holding out the object which was wriggling frantically and squeaking very angrily "LET ME GO!"

"Pickle here is a fairy always into mischief - aren't you Pickle?" "I AM NOT!" Pickle answered crossly, stamping her foot.

'Say sorry to Mr Wormchuck please Pickle." "WILL NOT!" replied an angry Pickle, Mummy opened her pocket and dropped Pickle in. "We will talk later."

Mr Wormchuck let me apologise on behalf of Pickle for getting caught up in your nose. That couldn't be very pleasant for either of you. However you really must go home. You are nearly as big as our garden and I don't know how to explain you to anyone as not many people have very big purple worms in their gardens, they tend to be pink....and...erm...small and definately not with pink and green hair, so you can see the problem. You are of course welcome back, when we can prepare the garden to hide you, bring along Mrs Wormchuck too."

Lilac broke off.

"Good bye for now Mr Wormchuck."

"Giant worm, dear giant worm, it's not your time here and no harm done, so go back home and don't be glum."

Lilac quickly clicked her fingers, 'POP!' Mr Wormchuck vanished. Marmalade looked sad.

Ebony was as still as a statue, she had discovered both Mummy and Marmalade could do magicky things.

Marmalade watched on fascinated keeping his eyes firmly fixed to the spot where a very annoyed and slimy Pickle climbed out of Mummy's pocket. "Oh you look delectably chase-able," he said, Pickle reached forward and smacked him hard on his nose, "try it," she threatened, she was in a vile mood. Ebony was quiet and crying softly. 'What a Saturday afternoon,' Mummy thought, out came the fairy dust. Pickle was still in a very shouty mood "That stuff DOES NOT work on me, you go away and leave me alone! IT'S YOUR FAULT I'm covered in this stuff Manky Marmalade and it's horrible!" Pickle stamped her foot again folded her arms with a HUFF, showing everyone just how very cross she was. "Shush now, you are having some," Mummy sprinkled Pickle and then more over Ebony and Marmalade. "We will all feel better very soon, less shouty and calmer, I hope," muttered Mummy quietly.

Marmalade's cat instincts had kicked in, he watched Pickle wriggle, fighting an urge to bop her with his paw, she looked like a mouse to him, reaching out he pulled his paw back ready to make a big bop, an extra big wriggle from Pickle and Marmalade let fly. Mummy caught his paw. Pickle was shouting even louder now "you, you BIG FAT OLD MANKY SMELLY GINGER TOM!!" Pickle was furious. Silence hit the air. Marmalade's face dropped. Pickle knew she had gone too far but HE wasn't the one covered in stinky green bogey sparkling slime it wasn't HIS wings stuck together. "ENOUGH!" Mummy snapped, Marmalade LEAVE Pickle alone, she was annoyed, Pickle we DO NOT name call, do we?" Pickle was in the baddest of bad moods. Marmalade was trying not to laugh, she did look all the world like a wriggling mouse and he still badly wanted to chase her. Pickle bopped Marmalade hard on his nose with her wand, "OUCH!" Marmalades paw began to rise, Mummy looked at him and gave him a wag of her finger, "YOU STINK, NOT ME!" Marmalade shouted at Pickle. He wasn't wrong.

"So, Pickle, what were you doing to get caught up inside Mr Wormchucks nose?"

"I wanted to say hello to him and apologise on behalf of Marmalade for bringing him here, it was his fault he was here do you know that Queen Lilac?" Mummy looked at her puzzled, "you usually call me Mummy, why change today?"

"Mummy was still looking at Pickle, "do you know I was just about to send him home to Worm World? Until you sneezed I had no idea you were inside his nose. It would have been very difficult to get you back home safely again." Pickle mumbled, "sorry Mummy."

A distant memory stirred again inside Marmalades mind.

"Right, let's get that slime off you Pickle, we need to clean your wings first as we don't want them getting damaged. First things first though. Marmalade you already know Pickle and believe me you do, Ebony you don't, holding out a now very quiet Pickle on the palm of her hand Mummy showed her to Ebony. Pickle knows you well, she is a friend. A bit of a mischief making fairy but loving and kind all the same. Hey Pickle?" Marmalade piped up "Pickle is always in a pickle! Or is she a cheese and pickle sandwich? Or maybe pickle soup or pickle juice?" 'Hahahaha he roared with laughter, waving his paw in the air,' once again, Marmalade thought he was very funny.

"Right let's sort your wings otherwise you won't be flying anywhere."

Ebony sat down rather too quickly. "Ebony, are you alright?" Ebony was sure everything was ok, she was just as sure everything wasn't ok.

Daddy had woken up from his faint and went to get himself a glass of water, leaning against a door he had been watching his family he was feeling strange again, he wanted a cup of tea but a bigger part of him never wanted a cup of tea ever again. Fairies though? Fairies being washed in the kitchen sink because they had been stuck inside a gigantic worms nose? He started feeling really woozy and with a thump down he went again - Daddy had fainted again.

"Oh dear, Daddy does faint a lot, let me sort him out. Pickle please stand still for a moment - a big ask I know!"

Pickle stuck her tongue out at Marmalade, waving her wand at him. Marmalade was teasing her, how does it feel to be covered in green slime, is it a new beauty treatment? Did she feel like a big mousey, stinky, slimy bogey? That was what she looked like. On and on they argued. Mummy wondered wearily if these two were ever going to get on? Ebony held up her hand. "Stop" a calmness surrounded them.

Lilac with a large pinch of fairy dust sprinkled it over her husband Arthur as he slept on in a faint.

Pickle and Marmalade had become far too quiet. 'What where they doing now?' she wondered, turning around again she discovered they were hugging each other, like long lost friends.

Mummy sat down, reached inside her pocket, drew out a very large pinch of fairy dust and sprinkled it over her own head, she was exhausted from all the shocks, surprises, tears and arguing and right now she needed one of those self filling cups of tea.

The next morning Ebony had something on her mind as she sat down for breakfast Mummy noticed how quiet she was. "Is everything alright only you don't look happy?" Ebony didn't reply instead she picked up the spoon in front of her. Ebony wanted to ask Mummy so many questions, she didn't know where to start, everything had suddenly become very strange.

Mummy poured a lovely big bowl of treacle porridge into Ebony's bowl, added a dash of fairy dust, did the same for Marmalade, gave them both a reassuring hug and passed them a jug of cream.

As always, the fairy dust made Ebony and Marmalade feel happy and at ease.

"Mummy, how did Daddy know about a gigantic purple worm? How? How did he know it had long green and pink hair? It's not like you can guess something like that is it?" Mummy looked at Ebony and thought for a few moments. "A few years ago, I met Mr Wormchuck, I went out very late at night putting the hens to bed. Mr Wormchuck was hiding, as you can imagine, being the size of a small bus you are never going to be able to hide easily. He was hiding up a tree." Ebony and Marmalade laughed, "he wasn't up a tree, don't be silly Mummy!" Mummy laughed too, "I swear honestly he was up a tree, he lost his grip and fell, landing with a massive splat. I didn't know what to do apart from see if he was alright. He had winded himself badly and started to breathe quickly, before you know it, he had sniffed me into his nose. That is how I know about the slime and how I know how badly it smells. I was so embarrassed and wasn't sure if I was dreaming, I saw my camera, grabbed it and took a photo. Mr Wormchuck is a really dear old worm, very polite and sweet, he would never hurt anyone.

I asked him why he was in our garden, he explained to me that one of the fairies had been making tricks with her wand, she had been mixing up a spell, she thought she was being very funny, before he knew it, instead of sitting having a cup of tea doing his crossword in Worm Weekly Magazine with Mrs Wormchuck BANGCRASHPOP! he was stuck up a tree and not quite sure how he was going to get down until he fell down, which looking on the bright side, at least solved one of his problems." Ebony and Marmalade were spellbound. "Some cameras can develop the photograph straight away, the one I had did. I wondered how I could hide the photo from Daddy. Mr Wormchuck came up with the idea to say it had been someone who was in fancy dress costume that had stopped to ask for directions. I hid the photo in the kitchen drawer underneath the spoon tray. I never gave it another thought, I never thought Daddy would see it, clearly he has although he has never said anything about it."

Chapter 11

Ebony We Are All Fairies.

"Mummy, you can do magic can't you?"

"Yes Ebony, we all can, even you, even Marmalade, Pickle usually gets herself into trouble and we tend to end up rescuing her quite a lot, she is very accident prone. We are all fairies of one kind or another she added looking directly at Marmalade."

Marmalade had been gulping his porridge and now looked hungrily at his empty bowl. "Would you like some more Marmalade?" Marmalade looked delighted nodding as Mummy poured him another very full bowl of treacle porridge. Mummy was relieved to see Marmalade had not put an outfit on. "You look so much better today Marmalade, good to see that wonderful orange fur." Marmalade blushed his fur turning a deep crimson red. " Didn't I look snazzy though?" he tilted his head and grinned.

"We are fairies and can all do fairy magic." Ebony repeated this many times. "I did tell you I felt if I waved my paw around something would happen I did say, that's how we got into trouble." Marmalade looked at Mummy, suddenly his face was sad. Big tears welled in his eyes. "Mummy I am sorry I caused so much trouble yesterday. Please don't send me away. Please." Marmalade sobbed. He couldn't bare the thought of leaving his family, the family he loved so deeply, Ebony pulled him to her, Mummy wrapped her arms around both of them.

"Never in a million years Marmalade, you are our family, a son, here you will stay, with us, part of us, always." Marmalade smiled happily, tears gone. Purr, Purr, Purr. Sitting together they finished breakfast.

Chapter 12

A Sunny Day.

"What are you two doing today, it's such a lovely day?" "We are going to play in the garden Mummy, Marmalade wants to show me how to use the slide properly, I'm still not sure though. Can we have a picnic outside and get the paddling pool out please?" Mummy nodded, "Daddy is bringing fish and chips home tonight, It'll be nice to sit outside to eat them."

Their first thoughts were let's check the garden to make sure nothing is ready to jump out on us. You couldn't be sure of anything anymore, not after the past couple of days, they had been different to say the least. Nothing seemed out of place and nothing felt like it was going to happen. They sat down together. "Let's make a daisy chain." Marmalade looked at Ebony and waggled his paw at her, "not sure what a daisy chain is, but I don't have thumbs Ebony." Ebony picked up a daisy and showed it to him. "You have to pick it so the stem is as long as it can be and then you use your thumbnail to make a hole in the stem, oh yes, I see the problem now, she giggled." Ebony carried on showing Marmalade, "you keep doing it again and again," threading one daisy into another. "We can make a crown or a necklace." Marmalade was studying his paws, picking daisies and threading them together would be something he wasn't going to be able to do any time soon.

Ebony had given Marmalade the job of guarding the daisies, he wanted to pounce on them and chew them into tiny pieces. "I know Marmalade, you can model them, we can give this one to Mummy, let's go and find her."

"You look pretty in that necklace," Mummy smiled, Marmalade pulled the necklace from around his neck, "Mummy lower your head so we can put the chain on you please." Mummy was delighted. "How very pretty, thank you both. Before I forget, Mr and Mrs Wormchuck are coming over for dinner tonight I've also invited Mrs Wonders. We can eat at the bottom of the garden, we'll put sheets on the washing line and on all the trees, we'll put some lights on them, it'll stop people being able to see Mr and Mrs Wormchuck and it will also make it pretty." Ebony and Marmalade were delighted.

Ebony didn't know, she couldn't possibly know that dear old Mr Wormchuck had devoted the past 6 years of his life to guarding Ebony, even Mummy hadn't known until the night he had fallen from the tree.

The night Ebony was born was a very special and magical night, all the Animals and Insects and the all the Fairies and Flutterbees in fact, all of Queen Lilacs Fairy Kingdom Above and Below pledged to look after Ebony to keep her safe at all times.

When Mr Wormchuck had fallen out of the tree, he had actually being doing a security check of the garden as he had done every day since the day Ebony had been born. Mr Wormchuck didn't care to slither around on the ground, no, that was far to obvious, he liked to shimmer up a tree and leap from one tree to another then on to the next. In fact Mr Wormchuck was more like a monkey than a worm. Obviously all worms jump from tree to tree, how else were they supposed to carry out a security check? Anyway, it would be really rather silly to slither along the ground, no, not his cup of tea at all, no thank you!

"He won't sniff us in will he Mummy?" Ebony was very unsure, her hand reaching out for Marmalades paw. "I'm quite sure he won't sweetheart, but if he starts to sneeze, then move right out of his way, both of you, remind me to tell Pickle." Mummy crossed her fingers as she said this. Ebony noticed a glimpse of gold on Mummy's head, she has seen this before on Mummy, but has never seen anything more than a flash of gold. "Right, both of you back out to the garden and I'll bring you out an ice pop, first I need to make a phone call."

Mummy checked Marmalade and Ebony were safely outside, they had become best friends and were inseparable chattering away to each other.

"Pickle?" Mummy found that whenever she rang the fairies, somehow, Pickle was the fairy that answered the phone, every single time, before anyone else ever had a chance.

Pickle was a full blown chatterbox, she loved a good gossip with anyone and could start a conversation in an empty room. "Pickle please listen to me, firstly before I forget, Mr and Mrs Wormchuck are coming over for dinner this evening, please stay away from their noses." A not so small "huff" could be heard. "Now Pickle, I'm only saying, that is all. The reason I'm phoning and it is you I need to speak with is that Marmalade can make fairy magic easily and without a spell. He waved his paw around and summoned Mr Wormchuck as you know, although he doesn't know how he does it, so if he makes a spell would you please cancel it immediately, could you tell the others too?" Pickle agreed, she was an extraordinary little fairy, so full of mischief but also of love and compassion. She had seen Marmalade burst into tears when he mistakenly brought Mr Wormchuck here and secretly started to adore him.

Pickle and Marmalade had got off to a bad start arguing and bickering all the time. Ebony had done something, though what she did, Pickle didn't know, everything calmed down and soon Pickle and Marmalade were hugging each other. Remembering Mummy's face when she saw them hugging was very funny. She smiled. "I wasn't spying the other day Mummy, it is my duty to keep Ebony and now Marmalade safe and a gigantic purple worm is not safe. I was simply going to ask why he was here in the daytime. I see him all the time at night but there is never anybody out, Ebony is always in bed, so there's no chance of her being squished. I was checking him out, he had been admiring the flower bed, smelling the flowers,

I was behind one of them and whoosh, I was straight up inside his nose. I am sorry I caused trouble." Mummy knew Pickle ended up in a Pickle almost all the time, it seemed to be one of those things. "It's fine Pickle, these things happen, quietly and unseen she turned a funny shade of red, remembering vividly the inside of Mr Wormchucks nose."

Mummy went to the freezer and found them each an ice pop, they'll be lovely and refreshing, she thought. The day was very warm, she was tired and still had the paddling pool to inflate and fill. Maybe a little magic can help me out, sometimes she would make a small spell to help with the housework, mmm, let me think.

"Summer Magic please fill the pool, fill it with seawater and full of all things sea born, let it be shallow and warm, let them hear seagulls and boat bells, let them smell hot dogs, seaweed and sun cream, let it all be a happy beach dream." 'POP!'

That was some spell Mummy made. Mummy's magic was wonderful. If you looked at something and you weren't expecting anything other than what you were expecting to see, then that is all you would see. If you were expecting to see a donkey, nothing more than a donkey, then all you would get is a donkey, if you saw a slice of cake, but could imagine a cake shop, you would end up with a massive chocolate cake, next to an even bigger chocolate cake, next to a gigantic chocolate cake and on the top of that cake would be hundreds of pink sugar mice waving happily, singing and blowing strawberry bubbles. A wonderful kind of fairy magic indeed.

Lilac smiled, it was the best feeling in the world to be able to make fairy magic. She walked outside carrying the ice pops, she had thought to bring one for herself to share with Pickle. "We'll have lunch very soon, after lunch you can play in the paddling pool, you will both need sun cream on. I hope you like what I have done to the pool." "Cats do NOT wear sun cream!" said Marmalade rather haughtily. "You do," Mummy replied quickly, you are having some on your ears and your nose and that is all there is too it, they burn easily on cats, plus it's better to be safe than sorry." Marmalade looked embarrassed and apologised. He started to sniff the air, another deeply hidden memory stirred, "can I smell the sea?" He could hear popping and fizzing, Mummy blocked his view, she wanted them to have a wonderful surprise after lunch, his attention turned to his ice pop, "now that is lovely," the sea slowly slipped from his thoughts.

Marmalade had never had an ice pop before, he wasn't sure where he had lived before Ebony, he knew it must have been somewhere but couldn't remember where. He would ask Mummy another time, right now it didn't matter, he was happy.

"I'm going to make us all some tuna salad sandwiches, how does that sound to you both?" Ebony and Marmalade both nodded in agreement, there was that unexpected smell of sea air again surrounding them, fish sandwiches seemed the most perfect and exact thing to be eating, they were all suddenly very hungry.

"MMMM! Lovely sandwiches Mummy." Ebony and Marmalade said together. "It's been a really lovely day today hasn't it?" Ebony asked Marmalade. Marmalade smiled, he looked pale, worrying about something, he wasn't altogether sure he wanted to get wet, he hated water but he didn't want to let Ebony down. Mummy knew that once Marmalade was in the pool he would be fine, all his fears would vanish and a small sprinkling of fairy dust would solve the rest.

Mummy rubbed sun cream on Ebony and Marmalade much to Marmalades dislike, he kept stating very firmly cats do not wear sun cream, the more Marmalade licked, the further he spread it and the more matted his fur became, he was becoming really quite grumpy.

"Right off you go, I will be watching you both from the kitchen window. Pickle is watching you from her favourite hiding place," they turned and could clearly see a small smiling and waving Pickle, perhaps not such a great hiding place after all.

Chapter 13

The Paddling Pool.

"First in," yelled Ebony, she jumped in the pool and sat down with a large splash, she looked around, confused. She wasn't sure what she was seeing, but for sure it wasn't a paddling pool. "Marmalade get in and tell me what you see." Marmalade noted the doubt in Ebony's voice, he was a loyal friend, forgetting his dislike of all things water, jumped in next to her. Both looked around, they were seeing a rock pool, shallow one side, deeper in the middle and deeper still a little further out so they could swim. The smell of the sea was wonderful. Marmalade was watching the water very closely.

"Come here little fishy and get into my belly." Marmalade was jabbing the fishes, trying hard to spear one with his claws. Mummy had made sure he wouldn't be able to hurt one, although she wasn't planning on telling him.

Pickle loved paddling pools, flying over and landing on Ebony's shoulders she looked around very impressed by the beautiful rock pool before her, Mummy had done an amazing job. The smell of sea air and a soft warm breeze made Pickle feel very sleepy, flying down to a small rock she laid down, Pickle drifted into a very deep sleep. Ebony jumped as more and more tiny fishes gathered around her toes. "EEEEEEEEKKKK, I don't like that! Tell them to stop Marmalade, tell them that!" Bubbles fizzed around them. "Hello," they called, "Hello Princess Ebony, come swim with us," one called out. Ebony and Marmalade were surprised, "did you just say hello?" Ebony asked one of the fish, "yes, why wouldn't I?" The fish answered back, "erm…" Ebony replied. "We are Fairy Kingdom Below Fish, we know you both, my name is Blue, probably because I'm blue and probably because they'd run out of names by the time they'd got around to choosing mine." Giving them a shrug and a smile Blue carried on. "Hello Marmalade, are you still telling awful jokes?" Marmalade shook his head, this was all just too much for him, he splashed his paw down hard into the water sending splashes and waves around the pool. "I haven't got a Cats Notion as to what you mean!" Marmalade blushed a violent crimson red.

"Come on both of you," called out Blue, "there is someone who would love to meet you again." Ebony hold Marmalades hand, Marmalade you hold my tail, no pinching though," he added grinning.

Blue took a very big deep breath, pulling Ebony and Marmalade down into the water. Shallow at first, then suddenly very deep and crystal clear. Blue as blue could be, around them seaweed was drifting in the current as if waving to them. Crabs waved their claws in greeting, starfish danced on two legs, more and more fish joined in. It had become a parade, on and on they swam as Pickle slept on.

"Where are you taking us Blue?" Asked Ebony, she hadn't realised she was breathing and talking underwater. "There are people who want to meet you Ebony. They don't often get the chance." Wanting to add, 'until I made Pickle fall asleep,' but quickly deciding to keep that to himself.

"I promise you, you do not have anything to worry about."

On they swam, until a dark shadow in front of them began to look like the entrance of a cave.

Ebony and Marmalade were now standing inside, the rocks were slippery, Blue was standing, walking on his tail, all fish do this when they think no one is looking. "Princess this is an honour for us. Please come forward and meet someone who is also very special." Ebony was holding Marmalades paw tightly, she was scared and also not scared, however she wasn't going anywhere without him.

Sea water dripped from the ceiling....plop...plop...plop, "don't worry about that," Blue smiled, "we do need it to be a little wet in here as we all live underwater."

Slipping and sliding they moved forward, it reminded Ebony of walking on ice. Marmalade had grasped Ebony's hand very tightly, he was scared though he wasn't going to let Ebony see, he was going to keep her safe.

Chapter 14

Neptune.

Soon they were in a room at the back of the cave, it glowed a beautiful sea green, there in the middle of the cave, stood a golden thrown, sitting upon it was an old man with a very long and tangled beard, two crabs could be seen playing hide and seek within it. The man wore a crown and was holding a long golden spear. He looked at Ebony and smiled kindly "hello Ebony, hello Marmalade my dear old friend, how splendid of you both to call in, come closer and talk with me."

"You are probably wondering who I am?" The old man turned to Ebony first. Ebony nodded, trying not to show how scared she was. Turning to Marmalade the old man asked "are you still telling your awful jokes?" He winked at Marmalade who blushed from head to toe, he had no idea who this old man was or why people kept asking him about his jokes, as far as he knew he only told good jokes and made some magic, though he wasn't allowed to do any magic if Mummy, Pickle or any of the other fairies weren't with him, where was Pickle anyway?

Marmalade started to ask the old man what he meant. "Excuse me Sir, why does everyone keep asking me about my jokes?" The old man smiled kindly and stroked Marmalades head. "You are the sweetest, most loyal and loving cat I have ever had the pleasure to know. What you were once you were made to forget to make it easier for you to settle in Fairy Kingdom Above. You will keep getting flashes of things from your past, all will become clear dear little soul." Marmalade was now even more confused.

The old man's beard was jumping around, with an ancient hand he picked out a crab, talking directly to one in particular, whispering something in to his ear. The crab fell silent immediately.

Plates and cups could be heard being loaded on to a tray, the most delicious aroma of hot steaming food tickled at their noses, they had not realised how hungry they were.

"How would you like to play a game? I haven't played a game in a very long time." "Yeeess, sir." Ebony stammered looking at Marmalade with a how does he know us look?

"Sir," Marmalade asked, "how do you know Ebony and I?" Marmalade asked. The old man rubbed his beard, the crabs had started to argue again and were snapping angrily at each other, dangling one from his fingertips, "I have asked you two to behave when we have company" he told the crab, pushing him back into his beard, further away from the other, "brothers you see," as if this explained everything to Ebony and Marmalade, "they argue and fight all the time."

"Sir, what should we call you?" "Well...erm," what should he say, he didn't want to scare either of them, nor did he want to tell them the truth, that was down to Queen Lilac and his son, Prince Arthur.

"Well I think for now you ought to call me Neptune. Just Neptune, if that is alright with you both?"

Neptune stood up and moved a large shell to the front of them, perfect for using as a table. Tea and hot seaweed cake had arrived, lovely lush looking seaweed sandwiches were also on the tray, it was a truly scrumptious feast, one that we could say was 'fit for a King.'

Blue walked forward. "Your Majesty, please sit, I will pour the tea and serve our wonderful guests." Turning to Ebony and Marmalade, he lowered his eyes, "please don't be cross with Pickle, I made her fall asleep." Marmalade looked at Blue, suddenly he was angry, very angry. "If you have put Princess Ebony in any danger I WILL EAT YOU," he roared.

Neptune held his hand out, immediately everyone calmed. Marmalade had seen Ebony do the same thing when he and Pickle were arguing, he looked puzzled. "No one is in danger Marmalade, Blue does Queen Lilac know where Ebony and Marmalade are?" Blue shook his head. "No King Neptune Sir, I'm very sorry," he looked sad and upset, he hadn't thought about that, getting rid of that pesky fairy had been his only thought. He had met Pickle numerous times, he knew how mischievous she was.

The food was served, it was as delicious as it had both looked and smelled, Marmalade stopped eating, he suddenly realised they were having tea with a King.

"King Neptune," Marmalade nudged Ebony. "KING NEPTUNE," he said again, not so quietly this time. "KING," nudging Ebony again.

"How are Lilac and Arthur?" Neptune asked, "I haven't seen Arthur for ages!"

"King Neptune," Marmalade started to say, "KING Neptune!" Marmalade more or less shouted the King bit. Ebony looked at Marmalade, she had finally caught on. "May I say what a delight and honour it is to meet you, thank you for allowing us to stay for tea, it has all been rather lovely." Ebony thought and then thought harder. 'King Neptune is very important, he knows Mummy and called Arthur his son. "King Neptune, Arthur is my Daddy's name, does that mean my Daddy is your son?" Neptune decided to ignore the question.

"Princess Ebony and Marmalade I am delighted to have had you here, shortly it will be time for you to leave. You must tell Mummy and Daddy you have been here and please tell them in no way was this Pickle's fault. Pickle's in a Pickle yet again," he chuckled.

There is it again, someone calling me 'Princess. I guess he's just being nice, thought Ebony.

"Have we all finished our tea and cake?" Neptune asked. He patted crumbs on to his lap, the two brother crabs grabbed at them gobbling them as quickly as they could trying to out eat the other. "Take no notice of Ross and Herbert, I've had quite enough of them today," both crabs were held up, "if you two do not stop arguing I will take you to, you know where." Both crabs immediately sat down, folded their legs, tucked their pincers in and were sat like a Saints with a very faint glimmer of a halo over each head.

Marmalade burst out laughing. That was one of the funniest things he had ever seen.

"Time for some games." Neptune called, "come on let's play merry go round with the lovely long armed Amy Octopus, everyone take hold of one of her hands and hold tight." Amy wrapped her long arms around them and held them tightly, she loved joining in games and this was one she did very well. She lifted them high up into the air, swinging them around, upwards, backwards, round and round, they laughed and laughed. Finally Amy stopped and placed them down. "Thank you Amy, that was brilliant fun, thank you." They were delighted. Amy blushed, thank you Princess Ebony, Marmalade," then sliding quietly back into the pool nearby.

"Princess Ebony and Marmalade it is time for you to leave us. Please say hello to Queen Lilac and Arthur for me. Would you ask them if they care to visit? I haven't had so much fun in such a very long time, thank you both." Neptune bent forward and kissed the top of their heads, hugging them. "Stay safe little ones, goodbye for now." Tears started rolling down Neptune's cheek. "Blue take them safely home please." Blue held their hands and walked them out of the room, back into the slippery cave and then finally into the sea to start their long swim home.

They held on tightly to Blue, he swam faster and faster. They were so big next to him. A thought suddenly occurred to Ebony, 'is this how Mr Wormchuck feels? We wouldn't ever hurt Blue, so why do I think Mr Wormchuck will hurt us?'

Before they knew it they were sitting in the shallow end of the rock pool, Blue snapped his fins and Pickle started to wake up. "Good bye my friends," said Blue happily. "It has been truly a pleasure to meet you, please visit any time you would like," he placed a blue ring on Ebony's finger and one on Marmalade's paw, "do not ever take them off," blowing them both a kiss he swam off.

Ebony felt as if she had just woken up from a lovely long sleep, looking at Marmalade she noticed he was also yawning, so it had been a dream and nothing more, she thought to herself. Pickle sat up. "Did we all fall asleep?" She asked looking very guilty.

Ebony looked at her hand, seeing the blue ring she looked at Marmalade, he was also wearing a ring. It hadn't been a dream, Mummy and Daddy also had a similar ring.

Mummy had been watching Blue when he called on Ebony and Marmalade. She had known Blue for many many years and knew him well, Blue was a very honest and sweet little fish, she knew he would never get them into harm, he would look after them both always. She knew exactly where he would be taking them.

Mummy walked up to the paddling pool and sat down. "You both alright?" she asked smiling at them. Ebony nodded, nodding was the only way she could answer Mummy for the moment, thinking whatever she said they were bound to get into trouble.

"Mummy you always say, never go off with strangers." Ebony looked at her ring, it was such a beautiful blue, she held up her hand to show Mummy,' "a fish called Blue gave them to us."

"How is Neptune?" Mummy asked. "He's erm, he's fine," he asked we say hello to you and Daddy and to remind you to visit, he's very old Mummy."

"How do you know Neptune Mummy? Do you know he is a King?" Suddenly feeling it was the silliest question in all of silly land she wished it to be ignored. "Mummy they said to tell you none of this was Pickles fault, Blue did something to make her sleep." Mummy looked at a very embarrassed Pickle. "I know. I was watching. I do know Blue and yes I do know Neptune - King Neptune, I will explain another time. I knew you weren't in any danger whatsoever. I saw Blue placing a sleeping spell on poor Pickle, at least it was only to make her sleep and not anything else, I have seen him make some very naughty spells in the past, like sticking toffee apples to crabs pincers to make them look and sound like they were playing drums, the more the crabs tried to shake the toffee apples off, the faster the drum beat became, it was very funny, oddly enough the crabs never hurt anyone again."

"Daddy won't be long before he's home with fish and chips, our guests should arrive soon, it's been a very long day and I'm really looking forward to relaxing tonight." Marmalade's tummy rumbled in agreement. It felt like it was only a few moments ago they were enjoying seaweed sandwiches and seaweed cake, his tummy rumbled again, he was ready for dinner.

"Daddy's name is Arthur, isn't it Mummy?" Ebony asked. Mummy didn't answer. "Can we all visit Neptune again tomorrow, he did say it's been a very long time since he's seen you both?" "We will see," Mummy replied following it with a smile. "Right, time to start sorting out sheets and getting lights around the trees, we need to get the garden sorted for our guests."

Ebony and Marmalade were still sitting in the pool enjoying the smell of candy floss and hearing the seagulls calling out as they flew overhead, the warm gentle breeze on their faces was reassuring.

Chapter 15

The Steal.

Ebony reached over the pool edge, her hand scooping sand deciding to build a sandcastle. "Come on Marmalade, let's make a sandcastle, we can put a flag on the top, it'll be the best one there has ever been." They both began building, pulling and pushing sand this way and that, the castle started to take shape it looked wonderful. "Why don't we put shells on it?" Marmalade asked, "there were some on the ledge I noticed them when we swam past with Blue." Ebony agreed shells would indeed make the castle look the 'bee's knee's, although she had no clue what bee's knee's looked like, Daddy said it all the time, so it must be right.

Ebony reached over the pool edge, first her fingertips, then fingers and hand, her wrist and arm, reaching a bit further still, SPLASH. Ebony had vanished. Marmalade looked inside the pool, he couldn't see Ebony. "MMMMMMUMMMMYYYYY!" he screamed loudly, he had never been so frightened as he ran to her. "Ebony has fallen into the pool - I can't see her! She's disappeared!" Pickle had been watching as Ebony had fallen in the pool and vanished, Pickle thought she had been pulled in by someone or something no one had seen. Jumping straight in after her, Pickle could see no sign of Ebony, searching every ledge and every nook, there was no sign of her. Pickle remembered Ebony was wearing her blue ring, one that would keep her safe under water, Pickle swam faster than fast towards Neptune's cave.

Arriving quickly she leapt into the cave "Ebony has vanished! Someone grabbed her from under the water in the pool, she's gone, I can't find her anywhere," Pickle was shouting at top speed. Neptune raised his spear and slammed it down with a force so strong the whole cave shook. All fell silent. "Princess Ebony we are coming for you." An army of fish, crabs, squid, octopus, lobsters and pirates all followed Neptune as he jumped into the deep blue water and swam as fast as ever they could.

Marmalade ran back to the pool and without any further thought jumped in the deep end, he swam past Pickle who was coming back to tell Mummy that Neptune and his Army were searching for Ebony. Marmalade didn't care, he was going to look for Ebony and that was all there was too it.

Mummy was waiting for Pickle. "TELL DADDY AND SEND FOR HELP," she dived in tapping something on her wrist. It notified all Fairy Kingdom Above and Below of Ebony's disappearance. Help was most definately needed.

Pickle rang Mr Wormchuck, "please help us find her." 'BOOM, BANG, POP!" Mr Wormchuck was standing next to Pickle looking very scared. Pickle explained everything to him, he didn't like water but this was Ebony, his Princess, nobody was going to hurt her, ever. Pickle started to cry.

"Now, now Pickle, don't upset yourself dear, we will find her, you've been very brave telling Neptune, ANYTHING could have eaten you when you were swimming down there, you're so very small." Pickle went red. "ANYTHING can try." She muttered angrily.

SPPPPPLLLLASSSSH, Mr Wormchuck had dived into the pool and even though he was breathing in, he was well and truly wedged in stuck fast. "A little help here Pickle please?"

"The pool is too small, make it one size fits all," 'POP!' Pickle waved her wand, trying not to giggle.

Mr Wormchuck was in deep water, down and down he went. Pickle didn't know worms could swim.

Pickle watched, she knew the water held secrets, dark, menacing secrets. A place where bad pirates lived. A place where you had nothing. A place where you didn't dare sleep. A place where enormous oysters guarded their treasures eating anything that dared to venture near. A place you never ever wanted to be.

"HELP ME, HELP ME PLEASE!" This time there could be no mistake, it was definately his Ebony. "Ebony, where are you?" Marmalade called, "shout again!" Neptune and his Army had caught up, they all heard Ebony pleading for help, they were feeling incredibly helpless but together they were determined and strong.

Around them there were giant limpets and oysters, they were furious at being disturbed. Marmalade banged on one, "hello, may I say what a wonderful looking limpet you are, however we are here on very important and urgent business. Have you seen a small girl being dragged away, by whom we know not, but let's be honest, you wouldn't see a young girl being dragged away usually would you?" The limpet opened one eye, refusing to speak, he closed his eye again. Marmalade was furious, "I ASKED HAVE YOU SEEN A YOUNG GIRL BEING DRAGGED OFF A FEW MINUTES AGO?" Again one eye opened and then closed, sticking his tongue out at Marmalade for good measure. Marmalade Kung Fu kicked the Limpet, who remained firmly stuck with his eyes still closed. "Limpet, dear, old fella, kindly tell me who has taken Ebony and where or I WILL EAT YOU!" Limpets eyes opened. Neptune was pointing his spear at the limpet. "Tell me, I order you, or be smashed into thousands of pieces!"

Limpet started speaking quietly, very quietly at first, he knew if anyone heard him mention Ebony he would be smashed up anyway. The Sea Monster would eat him and he didn't think it would be in a garlic and wine sauce either.

"The Sea Monster has taken her, he's going to put her in prison and will torture her, to hurt you Marmalade, he wants you dead, he says you have unfinished business, that you took something of his, he wants it back desperately.   He heard you are now living Above and how happy you are living with Ebony, it didn't take him too long to figure out how to get your attention."

Limpet continued. "You will have to give back whatever it was you took, that's the only thing that will calm him otherwise he will truly enjoy hurting Ebony," he said speaking as seriously as ever a limpet could.

Marmalade was furious, Neptune grabbed him and held him back. "You are an absolute disgraceful coward for allowing a little girl to be dragged away, taken into the dark depths of who knows where, you absolute COWARD. I WILL BE BACK FOR YOU, MAKE NO MISTAKE!" Marmalade held his eyes in a death glare at limpet. "BE SURE OF THAT," he hissed.

Neptune held Marmalade, "do you remember taking anything from Sea Monster Marmalade?" Marmalade shuddered and shook his head. "No. I don't remember anything about living down here. Not a thing. Can't return what ever it is if I can't remember what I took, how do I get Ebony back if I can't remember?" Marmalade started to cry, Neptune stroked him. "My darling old friend, you need your memories back, with a flash of his hand Neptune whispered something and blew ancient secret words into Marmalades ear.

Marmalade, looked up, looking straight at Neptune. Memories were flooding back, waiting for the one memory that would show him what it was he had to return, now holding on to

Neptune as hundreds of memories flooded his mind. "AH GOT IT!" We have to get it and return it," Marmalade looked deeply unhappy, tears fell silently down as he swam further down into the dark menacing water. An enormous oyster was watching as Marmalade tried swimming past first one way then another, oyster flipped, turned and blocked Marmalade at every turn. "Let me open you, you stupid idiot." Oyster spurted water at Marmalade snapping at him, barely missing his whiskers. "I need your pearl, I put it in there years ago, for safe keeping, but now my Ebony is in serious danger, I have no alternative but to return it," he tried reasoning with oyster. "Nope," oyster refused. "Please!" Marmalade begged. "Nope," oyster shook his head. "Not happening. I hope you loose your friend forever, rot in pieces you fousty old ginger cat."

'SMMMMMASSSSHHHHH!' Oyster was gone, the sea cloudy an empty space where it had stood moments earlier. Mr Wormchuck had heard everything, being a man of action, jumped on oyster, picked him up and smashed him down. Oyster hadn't know what had hit him. When the water cleared, there stood a pearl. A golden pearl that shone brilliantly. Neptune looked at Marmalade, "I know, I understand." Marmalade nodded, "I need to give this to Sea Monster."

Marmalade picked up the pearl, tears rolled down his face, he lovingly stroked it, placing a kiss on it.

Off they swam. Marmalade, Neptune, the Army, Mr Wormchuck. Mummy had caught up.

They were swimming down to Davey Jones Locker. A dark and awfully sad place at the bottom of the sea.

Mr Wormchuck had ordered them all to hold on to him and hold tight. He was going to be the first in line, he knew he could withstand a big attack, the others looked so small and fragile, he couldn't or wouldn't let his friends get hurt.

Faster than a speeding boat they hurried on. The water darkened around them, colder than cold, misery everywhere surrounding them. Mr Wormchuck tapped his hair, a beautiful pink glow lit up around them, they didn't feel quite so scared.

Broken lobster pots, broken treasure chests, rotten seaweed, broken shells, empty rum bottles, smashed glass, broken crab shells littered the floor of the cave that was before them, topped up with despair and misery it was a truly horrid place, they had no choice but to go in, they all knew Ebony was in there.

The darkness grew darker, Mr Wormchuck turned the glow on his hair up, the glow really was a warming welcome to this menacing and nasty cave. They knew Sea Monster lived here. Blue swam up to Mr Wormchuck, "you are not alone my friend, we all stand together."

Chapter 16

Fight For Ebony.

The cave opened in front of them. "WHO DARES ENTER MY CAVE?" Boomed a voice, "Who are you?" No one answer the voice. "HOW DARE YOU ENTER MY CAVE, YOU NOW REFUSE TO SPEAK?" Sea Monster sounded terrifying. Mr Wormchuck was shaking, Marmalade was holding the pearl, Neptune had his spear ready, pushing Lilac behind him. Queen Lilac was not to be hurt under any circumstances.

"WHAT DO YOU WANT?" the voice boomed. Mr Wormchuck stood straight up, "Marmalade is here to return the pearl, we as his friends have accompanied him and we will be taking Ebony home."

"YOU dare threaten me? Marmalade stole the pearl from me, he trapped me and left me here, I heard he was in Fairy Kingdom Above. He left me to rot in this place, look what I have become. I was once a man, Marmalade stole my life from me, trapping me here, so, I ordered something of his be taken, something or someone of value to remind him exactly what he has done to me." He roared with laughter.

Marmalade moved forward, scared to his very paw endings. Standing high on his back legs he walked the last two paces at his highest height, holding out the pearl for Sea Monster. "Here it is, I am sorry, I don't remember you, I took it from

Henry not you, he can tell you why I took it, I haven't seen him for years, he was a really close friend, I don't know what happened to him. I had no idea I would be called up to Fairy Kingdom Above, I couldn't possibly have known, my memories were wiped, I couldn't remember anything."

"Where is Ebony, I demand her back now!" Marmalade hissed. "You stupid ignorant cat, you DARE to DEMAND anything from me, you are nothing more than an IDIOT!" Neptune had heard enough banging his spear down. Sea Monster laughed, "do you seriously think that you an old man, a woman, fish, sea food and this silly old cat can scare me, really?" He grabbed a hidden dagger.

Marmalade felt a tapping on his shoulder. Limpet stood looking at him "let me help, I am sorry for being a coward." Marmalade nodded thank you. Limpet stepped forward, the time to be scared was gone. He knew this could end badly, anyway he liked a good garlic and wine sauce he reminded himself. The largest and most powerful jet of water he could muster shot forward and hit Sea Monster full force, he fell backwards and dropped the pearl. It rolled towards Marmalade who rushed forward to grab it, Sea Monster plunged the dagger deep into Marmalade. Marmalade fell, laying motionless and quiet.

"MMMMmmmmm!! MUFFFFFFFFFF.....MUMMMMble!" Mr Wormchuck looked up, Ebony was glued to the ceiling she was screaming frantically, looking at Marmalade, her mouth had been clamped shut. "LEAVE HER!" Sea Monster demanded, "or I will cut you ALL into pieces."

"If you would like a go, then come on you vile thing." Mr Wormchuck was long since done with being scared. This thing that looked like a man made of broken lobsters and crabs and bits of shell with seaweed hanging from him, really wasn't anything to be scared of. "You, a grown - thing - whatever you are, bullying a little girl, planning to torture her, she's tiny and innocent and in no way could she fight you back, what on earth does that make you, you are utterly, shameful, you disgusting vile object." Limpet was shuffling backward, Mr Wormchuck moved blocking Sea Monsters view. Limpet had planned something.

Sea Monster rushed at Mr Wormchuck. Sea Monster was the size of a small car but Mr Wormchuck was the size of a bus. Sea Monster was made of all things broken and abandoned of lost hope of all bad things. He hadn't always been like this, this cave had made him meaner than mean, desperate to hurt anything, anyone and full of bitterness. Once upon a time he had laughed, once upon a time he had been magnificent. Then stupid Marmalade had trapped him in here and changed all of that.

Sea Monster clicked his claws together, he had another dagger.

"Ebony close your eyes," Mr Wormchuck was looking up at Ebony. He could see limpet inching up the wall, the plan suddenly becoming obvious to him, he didn't want Ebony to see what was about to happen next, she was still screaming, not taking her eyes off the lifeless body of her Marmalade.

"ATTACK!" screamed Sea Monster as he tried to plunge the dagger into Mr Wormchuck, missing he became enraged, the floor and walls of the cave covered in wave after wave of crabs, lobsters broken pirates and all things bad. Setting on Mr Wormchuck again, cutting at him, slashing at him, slicing him, hurting him. Neptune banged his spear down and pointed it at Mr Wormchuck, "PROTECT." A golden and green light surrounded Mr Wormchuck, the pinching and cutting stopped hurting, Neptune pulled the glow around his Army, Mummy, upwards over Ebony and limpet and finally over Marmalade. Poor dear sweet darling Marmalade.

Pickle was stood by the pool as Daddy arrived home with fish and chips. "DADDY, DADDDDYYY!" she flew into Daddy's face, screaming at him. Daddy had known Pickle well, he had to pretend not to know her, because of who he was, it needed to be kept secret, now his family were all in danger, the pretending had to stop.

Pickle was crying as she clung to Daddy, please hurry Daddy. Pickle jumped unseen into Daddy's pocket, jumping in he swam down and down, he knew exactly where he was going. The water became colder and darker, he met limpets and oysters, one of the limpets pointed in the direction of where the others had previously gone. Arthur nodded at them in thanks.

Finally he saw the cave. He swam in as far as he could and silently crept further forwards. A voice was booming. He could see Sea Monster attacking Mr Wormchuck, being cut over and over again, he was covered in the most awful rotting creatures, they were attacking poor Mr Wormchuck.

"Brave now are you worm, like being eaten alive do you?" Sea Monster boomed.

Daddy was standing in front of Sea Monster. "Remember me?" Looking at Sea Monster. REMEMBER ME?" he asked angrily. You vile loathsome piece of work. You still don't learn do you? Always full of jealousy and spite, vicious as no other. You took the soul of Marmalades mother, you have become the disgusting thing you always were." Mummy stepped forward. Daddy picked up a huge stone and threw it at Sea Monster, it hit him hard, making a loud cracking noise. "I remember you dear sweet little brother, yes laugh at me, look what I have become, it was all Marmalades fault, you all liked me until he arrived, he trapped me in here and left me to rot, it's all his fault." Pointing at Marmalades body, "well he won't be able to bother anyone anymore, poor little DEAD Marmalade." Arthur's temper could not be calmed, he raged like a tornado in a storm, picking up rock after rock, each one splitting Sea Monster open a little more.

Neptune walked forward. "It was I, I trapped you here. You hurt Marmalades mother, Sarah, my cat, the most beautiful loyal and loving cat, the best friend anyone could have, you tortured her for no reason then threw away her body like old rubbish, you trapped her soul inside the pearl. Blue brought her body home to me.

Blue found Marmalade after you had hurt him too, you thought you had killed him, enough was enough, you could no longer be my son. I trapped you here for eternity, in the hope you would regret the hurt you did, for you to learn to be a decent person, but look what you have become. Why did you need to behave so violently, so badly, what did Sarah, Marmalade and all the other animals you tortured purely for fun ever do to you?"

Daddy opened his hand, pouring from his finger tips a beautiful glowing streams of gold and green sparks, beautiful but lethal, he carefully aimed his hand at Sea Monster. "You've killed yet again, our darling Marmalade lies dead before you, yet even now you aren't happy." You dare to steal my daughter to hurt her on purpose, to hurt us all – she's your niece for heavens sake, look how badly you've hurt Mr Wormchuck - it's time for you to leave the Above and Below, for you to no longer be allowed to live within our Realms," turning to Neptune, "I am sorry father I have to end this monstrosity's life in our Realm, he has to be moved on." Neptune nodded silently. Gold and green sparks covered Sea Monster, fizzing, popping the bubbling noises became louder and louder.

Mr Wormchuck was lying on his side, covered in crabs and lobsters, he couldn't hold out any longer. "Goodbye my darling Mildred," he whispered quietly. Daddy knew he had to do something. Neptune stepped forward, pointing his spear at Sea Monster, together they lifted him, sending him into a violent spin, faster and faster still until finally exploding.

Turning to the rotting crabs and lobsters attacking Mr Wormchuck, "stop or you are next."

The attack became frenzied, Mr Wormchuck was completely unable to fight back, rotten crabs and lobsters were spinning and exploding, it was a grim stinking sight. Pickle jumped on Daddy's shoulder shooting stars out of her wand. "Take that and that!" For one so tiny, her might, power and will were enormous.

The pirates that had once joined in with Sea Monster were fighting alongside Neptune and Arthur, the cave fell silent, mounds of rotting and dead things lay silently.

Daddy was stunned to see how strong Pickle's magic was, she was crying holding Marmalades body, hoping against hope he would stand up and make a terrible joke, she made a ladder for Daddy to climb up for Ebony, using limpet telling him when to spurt water and where, what pressure was needed they soon had Ebony down. Ebony ran to Marmalade, picking him up, her tears falling on him, she collapsed, "Marmalade, my beautiful Marmalade," Daddy picked them both up, Pickle had scrambled up on to Daddy's shoulder, now sobbing for Ebony too, her Princess Ebony, it had all been too much.

All looked around, it was a vile, stinking mess, covered from top to bottom in guts, mess and shells. They had crushed thousands and thousands of lobsters, crabs and all things bad, being both completely outnumbered and overwhelmed, they had fought and fought bravely and hard, they were looking at each other unsure what to do.

Daddy held Ebony. "Shhhh, sweetheart, it's ok," tears rolled down her cheeks, she couldn't catch her breath. Mummy put her arms around all of them. "Let us sort Marmalade out, we cannot leave our darling boy like this any longer, we have to try get him back." Ebony still held Marmalade, she was inconsolable. "Fairy Kingdom Above and Below, I ask of your energies, knowledge, love and healing to bring Marmalade back to us. Please mend the damage done and return him to us I beg you." 'POP!' The spell had been made, there was only one more thing Mummy could do. Fairy seaweed cream, an incredibly magicky cream, one that mended all things, she rubbed it into Marmalades wound hoping and hoping and hoping some more, all she needed was to see was the smallest sign of life, to know Marmalade would somehow be alright and that her request had been granted.

"Arthur, I have to help Mr Wormchuck, he's been injured badly." Lilac waved her wand, Mr Wormchuck floated. "It's alright Mr Wormchuck, we will take you home however we need to sort your injuries out first, I have some more special seaweed cream." Mr Wormchuck smiled a tiny, weak smile, he knew she would never hurt him.

"Pickle, come help me please," Pickle flew over landing on her shoulder. "When I say 1, help me cover Mr Wormchuck in this cream. It stings like a thousand bee stings for 3 seconds. We will tell Mr Wormchuck to count to 3. It will hurt him although it will mend him.

Mr Wormchuck, please count slowly from 1 to 3 and on 3 we will apply the cream. It does hurt, I cannot say it doesn't but only for 3 seconds. Please count with us. Lilac nodded to Pickle 1 and... they worked their magic in the speed of light, covering him in cream.

"AAAAAAAAAAAAAARRRRRRRRRRRRRRRGGGGGGGGGGGGHHHHHHHHHHOOOOOOOOWWWWWWWWW!" The scream could be heard all through Fairy Kingdom Above and Below.

Ebony felt a tiny wriggle, she didn't dare breathe, there it was again and another, a paw stretched out "AAAAAAAAAAAAAARRRRRRRRRRRRRRRGGGGGGGGGGGGHHHHHHHHHHOOOOOOOOWWW! Who put that cream on me? I've had that stuff before, ouch, ouch, ouch!" Marmalade snuggled into Ebony, "why are you crying my Princess?" "Oh Marmalade, you're back, you are here, my Marmalade." Ebony burst into tears. Daddy, Mummy, Neptune and Pickle looked on all badly hiding the tears now streaming down their faces.

"Right work to do, come on Ebony let's help sort things out." Jumping down from her arms he first checked on Mr Wormchuck, who moments before him had screamed loudly too. "That's some cream Marmalade, they don't warn you how bad it is do they?" Asked Mr Wormchuck. Marmalade nodded in agreement, "I have had it before, I remember now, has Sea Monster gone now?" he asked. Sea Monster was once Henry, your friend Henry, he has been moved on. Hopefully where he has gone this time he can learn." Neptune walked up to Mr Wormchuck and Marmalade, "his badness finally rotted him through, he tried and nearly succeeded to kill you before, the same as he did your mother, he didn't succeed though, Blue found you very severely injured, he carried you home, he saved your life."

Marmalade noticed Blue was missing, searching everywhere he could not find Blue, he was no where to be found. "No, no, no, where is he?" Neptune was holding the tiny blue fish in his hand, he was laying still, no sign of life. "Marmalade, I'm afraid our little Blue has given his life to save Ebony. Marmalade was silent. Walking to Neptune, he held out his paw, "please pass him to me," Neptune carefully placed Blue in to Marmalades paws, they closed around the tiny lifeless of Blue. Whispering unheard words into his paws, golden green sparks circled Blue's tiny body, placing a gentle kiss on Blue he handed him back to Neptune. "Don't give up on him yet."

Daddy looked around once more, "you've all helped fight Sea Monster today, some of you are badly injured, some won't be returning home. I can only say thank you to all of you and to the pirates. We now consider you family. It is time for us to thank you properly. We will hold a party in our garden, everyone is welcome. One by one the pirates smiled, said thank you and jumped into the water.

"BLUE, YOU'RE ALIVE!" Neptune roared in delight. Blue stood up smiling, "of course, Marmalade you are simply amazing, thank you, Sir.

Neptune had never been so happy. His granddaughter was saved and Blue was alive, happy days.

Everyone seemed reluctant to leave, Blue feeling much better decided to offer to make tea and sandwiches for everyone but he added only when they had gathered back at Neptune's cave. This was all the prompting they needed for people to start leaving the wreck of a cave that used to belong to Sea Monster.

Pickle was checking Mr Wormchuck, you seem to be all mended now, how do you feel?" "I am aren't I? Oh thank you both of you, I didn't realise that I was such a coward." "YOU SIR are no coward, Mr Wormchuck, you are an amazing, wonderful and very brave worm. I am proud to call you my friend." Pickle flew on to Mr Wormchuck's huge face and hugged him as best she could. Queen Lilac waved her wand. "I bestow on you an Honour of Fairy Kingdom for Bravery without Limits or Boundaries and for being prepared to lay your life down to protect Ebony, I make you here and now a Lord of Fairy Kingdom, Above and Below." 'POP!' stars flew out of her wand and surrounded Mr Wormchuck, he now wore a secret fairy crown. "We need to go back to Neptune's cave and have some of the lovely tea and sandwiches that Blue makes. He also needs a reward."

They took one further look around the cave, they all shuddered, Queen Lilac picked up the pearl, she noticed a split in it, it was wriggling in her hands, something was inside. Placing it safely in her pocket they all dived into the pool in which the pirates had jumped only a few minutes earlier, they too need a reward for their bravery.

The pirates were waiting for Queen Lilac, Mr Wormchuck and Pickle, they wanted to say 'good bye.' Waving their rotten hats at them, more raggedy bits than hat and expecting them to swim past they were taken aback when Queen Lilac swam towards them. "Please come to a party we are going to hold, you are all guests of honour, for showing bravery and courage and for this, 'POP!' stars and sparks surrounded the pirates. The curse which has lain on you has been ended. You are all free to go. Where you go is up to you. If you step on to land, you will become whole again. If you walk into water you will breathe like a mermaid, you will never loose your body again, it will remain whole. You will succeed in whatever you choose to do, but whatever you choose to do must be for the good. Firstly though, I really would be honoured if you would attend our party, we will send word when it is. You will be able to enter our garden through the pool which is already set up and ready. Thank you my friends. I hold you in my heart." Mr Wormchuck, Pickle and Queen Lilac waved, turned and left quickly. The pirates were smiling. Pirates don't smile usually.

As they drew near to Neptune's cave the sound of teacups clinking brought a very welcome thought of seaweed tea, very refreshing and warming. Everyone was sat around, they were comparing cuts and wounds, some were very deep and needed seaweed cream. 'How to do this for everyone and quickly so that they can all scream together?' Queen Lilac almost laughed then decided Pickle would be needed again. "So Pickle we will surround them all in a spell and on the count of 3 they can all have seaweed cream put on them together. It's going to be noisy."

"Right one moment everyone, hello can you all hear me? Yes? Good, now please put all your cups, saucers, plates and anything else you may be holding down on the floor and turn to face me please." Pickle had been dashing around laying trails of stars covering everyone in the cave. "Please count to 3 with me, this won't hurt a bit." Mr Wormchuck let out a loud chuckle. Queen Lilac looked at him. "Right then," signalling to Pickle once more, "let's count backwards from 3 to 1, everyone ready? 3... Queen Lilac pointed her wand, so did Pickle 'POP, BANG!' the cave lit up in beautiful stars flying around covering the injured, at the very same time a loud roaring and howling started up, the sound was heard miles away, seconds later everything was quietening down. Marmalade was holding Ebony, Neptune was talking with Arthur, Blue was happily serving some special sea pearl tea. One by one, the pirates entered the cave. "Everything alright Queen Lilac, only we heard screaming?" "Everything is fine, they've just been healed, now it's your turn?" Looking at the rotten bodies of the pirates, Queen Lilac knew 3 seconds would not cover it this time. "I'm not going to lie and say it'll be 3 seconds as the cream has so much more work to do. I think we are looking at around 20 seconds. That is a long time to be in pain, but we are all here for you." Queen Lilac whispered to Pickle, "let's stand them in a circle, we'll both cover them in layers and layers of stars, hopefully if Neptune joins in we can make it quicker still." Marmalade saw what Mummy was planning to do, he pulled at Daddy and walked over to Mummy, "I think we can help." Opening his paw sparks came streaming out. The pirates were well and truly covered in stars and sparks. "Everyone count to 20 with them. She winked at Pickle, 1 and NOW!" Pickle, Queen Lilac, Marmalade and Daddy let the stars and sparks work their magic. The cream turned the pirates green, despite their best efforts all were screaming, 20 seconds was feeling like a life time to them, they had been brave once, they would be brave once more. Ebony felt the itching in her palms again, she shrugged and opened her hand, holding it out towards the pirates. An incredible sense of both calm and peace surrounded them, it was helping them. Neptune watched her, this was his granddaughter, she had been given his Gift, he was delighted, there would be an array of things to teach her another time.

The screaming stopped, the pirates now looked like men rather than pieces of the rags and bones they had become living in Davey Jones Locker. The pirates looked at each other, they were whole. The magic had worked and now they looked splendid, hair beautifully tied back, brand new clothes and boots, freshly shaven, clean new teeth. How amazing did they feel?

"Stay and have some special pearl tea and seaweed cake." Blue addressed them. Queen Lilac looked down at Blue. "What can I give you, that you don't have already? You have courage, your body is healed, you are clever, loving and very brave. You should be rewarded." She thought and thought and came up with an idea.

"Make this fish one so dear one so little stand as man when he takes a step on land." 'POP!' Blue nodded his thanks. "I've never being able to walk on land before!" Once more he began serving tea and cake to the men who had been rotting pirates not a moment before.

"Marmalade, Mummy called for him, come here I have something for you." Marmalade pulled Ebony over with him, holding her hand they both approached Mummy together. "Yes Mummy?" Mummy was smiling. "Marmalade, I believe this is yours." She held the pearl out for him. Marmalade smiled, a beautiful gleaming smile, taking the pearl carefully, he rubbed his paws over it and placing a kiss on it. He noticed the split. The pearl was starting to disappear. Mummy and Ebony looked on. "What are you doing?" They both asked together. "This needs this to be guarded and hidden for now, until the right person can open it. I'm sending it back to be looked after by Fairy Kingdom Below." What is inside the pearl," asked Mummy? Marmalade started crying, My mother, Sea Monster wanted it to smash it, he...he...thought I had taken his Above Life from him, but I didn't do that, he became so mean and nasty he started turning into that monster, he killed my mother and stole her soul, locking her in the only thing that could hold her, this pearl, he kept taunting me, telling me he was going to smash it in front of me, that's why I had I had to take it, to hide it, to keep my mother's soul safe until we can open it. Fairy Kingdom Below warned me Sea Creature was making death threats to me, he was desperate to get the pearl back just to smash it out of pure evilness. I needed to keep my mother safe, I asked oyster if he would look after the pearl, after all you hide something in plain sight right? He was over the moon and took his work very seriously. When it came time to give the pearl to Sea Monster for Ebony's life, even then the oyster wouldn't let me have it back. Unfortunately the oyster no longer lives, I feel terrible, he was only doing his job."

"You and I will swim down to him, let's take the fairy seaweed cream and try to mend him, so once again he can guard your pearl. You were prepared to sacrifice your mothers soul to keep Ebony alive and safe. I can not thank you enough, my darling, darling furry son."

Quickly they swam down, some of the pirates decided Queen Lilac and Marmalade needed escorting. Darker and darker it became. Marmalade guided them to the huge gap that was once the oyster. Picking up some fragments of smashed shell, Marmalade looked embarrassed. "This was him." Looking at Mummy, he held his head low. "I'm sorry." Mummy touched his shoulder, "it's alright, you were just looking out for Ebony, we can rebuild him." Pickle crawled out of Mummy's pocket, "me help too."

"Well we can't warn him how badly this will hurt, can we?" "You can give it a go," mumbled a piece of shell. No one was expecting that. "Oyster, this will sting, but not for long." Knowing it was going to be even longer than the pirates, Queen Lilac rather conveniently forgot to mention this.

They collected as many pieces of the oyster as they could and placed them in a circle on the sea floor. Pickle had managed to smear the cream on to most of the pieces.

"Stars work your magic, make this spell, do it quickly and make him well." 'POP BANG!' Howling sounded out all around them as hidden pieces of shell darted past, oyster was swirling forwards and backwards, round and round, they could all see him mending. Finally the howling stopped and before them stood a magnificent oyster, beautifully mended and gleaming gold. A fitting tribute to an oyster that had been so loyal and had done it's job so very well, laying his life down to guard the pearl so carefully.

"WOW" they all said together, you look beautiful." Oyster was over joyed to be one whole piece again. "Thank you, I thought that was me done for, that I'd be like that forever, smashed and forgotten." Marmalade stepped forward and waved his paw in a circle, the pearl re-appeared. "This is for you to look after again, you know who it is in it, I believe you love her as much as I do, until the time is right please hold her safely. "No one will be able to prise her from me, I have made sure of that. I will protect her until that time Marmalade." Oyster opened his mouth, Marmalade placed the pearl inside. Snapping his mouth shut tightly, Marmalade knew she would be safe, he waved a sad farewell.

"Thank you, oyster, now we must be heading back, children to feed and get to bed and all that you understand." Oyster had no clue what Queen Lilac meant, never having fed a child or seen a child being put to bed but nodded anyway.

Safely re-entering Neptune's cave, Ebony had fallen asleep over Daddy's shoulder. Time for everyone to head home.

Mummy looked at Marmalade, putting her arms around him she lifted him up into a much needed cuddle. Poor sad, brave, loyal, loving Marmalade.

Goodbye's quickly over and with the promise of a party, everyone went their separate ways.

They climbed out of the pool together. Mrs Wonders was waiting for them all. Reaching into her pocket she covered everyone in fairy dust, it always helped, always. One of the pirates had followed the group home, he wanted to be sure they were safe. He too received a sprinkling of fairy dust. Mrs Wonders invited him to dinner. Fish and chips all round. He had never had anything like that before, he had been delighted to stay. He thought Mrs Wonders looked really pretty. He had taken a shine to her.

Everyone sat down, Mr Wormchuck had been granted the gift of being able to make himself larger or smaller as he so wished, and also to be able to control his slime output, which delighted him. He was currently Daddy size and sitting on the sofa alongside everyone else.

Mrs Wonders heaped piles of chips and fish onto everyone's plate, no matter how much she took from the bag Daddy had brought home, there were plenty left. Pirate had eaten his quicker than anyone else, he looked around "sorry, it's been a long time since I've eaten anything." Mrs Wonders quickly filled his plate again, he smiled shyly at her, his eyes followed her everywhere.

Mrs Wonders looked at them all, they all looked exhausted. "Firstly Marmalade, Ebony and Pickle are going for a bath in some BubblyWubblyFoam, sorts out all sorts of problems. Mr Pirate would you like a hot bath? We can make up a bed for you on the sofa. Lastly Lilac and Arthur you two can bathe last and then go straight to bed. I will sort everything else out."

One by one they bathed, all enjoying the extra softness of the BubblyWubblyFoam. Ebony, Marmalade and Pickle went straight to sleep after crawling into bed. Holding each others paw and hand. Pickle had curled up between them snuggling deep down into Marmalades long soft warm fur. All three were guaranteed a peaceful night with dreams of candy floss and bouncing on soft clouds. Mrs Wonders watched them from the door, blowing them a kiss she quietly closed the door and walked back downstairs. Pirate was delighted to be having a bath, it was something he had never done before. Mrs Wonders explained about taps and plugs, about warm towels, soap about toothbrushes and toothpaste. She had secretly added BubblyWubblyFoam and fairy dust to his already running bath. Closing the door, he suddenly announced, "my name is Sidney." It had been many, many years since he had said his own name out loud.

Mrs Wonders asked Mr Wormchuck if he'd like a bath, but he felt it was time to go home and explain the day to his wife. "Would you be so kind as to magic me home please Mrs Wonders?" He queried, Mrs Wonder nodded and with the click of her fingers Mr Wormchuck vanished.

"I've made a bed up on the sofa in the other room for Sidney, that is the pirates name by the way. He'll go straight to bed when he's out the bath. You two need to go to bed after your baths too, you look exhausted." Mrs Wonders blew a kiss at them and left.

Chapter 17

The Day After. The Day Before The Party.

Sidney was sat in the kitchen when they all came down after a most wonderful nights sleep any of them had ever had.

Mummy and Daddy had talked long into the night. They talked their secrets through. Daddy had a Fairy God Mother Witch as a Mother in Law, though he was really very fond of Mrs Wonders. Queen Lilac had King Neptune as her Father in Law, she too adored him, they had decided he needed to be included into Ebony's life and were working out ways to do this.

Mummy had decided it was a morning for hot and creamy sweet cinnamon porridge, followed by masses of toast with butter and of course marmalade, sweet, thick, sticky orange marmalade, gorgeous on hot buttered toast.

Everyone was enjoying their porridge, Pickle was sitting on Sidney's shoulder as she ate hers, she had noticed his fondness for Mrs Wonders and was watching him keep taking glances at a photo of her. Sidney was completely unaware of Pickle who was currently constructing good mischief.

The toast was chewed and crunched with lashing of butter and marmalade making it all so very delicious. Marmalade thought he was hilarious as they were eating his name he started to joke around, "oh no, that's my leg, now you're eating my arm, no, no, no, that's my ear and it hurts, ha ha ha!" Ebony went very pale and asked for strawberry jam instead.

"So, the party, we have agreed to put a marquee in the garden, we can ask the trees if they would mind moving for a day or so, I'm sure they will agree, they are kind old things. Cheerypops has offered to make all the food, which is wonderful. Candy floss will be making itself in one corner, hot dogs in another, food enough for everyone. We need music, Sidney has offered the service of his pirate friends, they sing really well apparently."

 "Enchantments will be placed all around the garden so no ordinary person will be able to see, hear or even smell anything different than what they usually would. Camp beds are to be placed all over the garden for the guests who decide they would like to stay the night. The only other thing then are drinks. "What would everyone drink?" Mummy asked. "Not a problem my dear," Mrs Wonders said as she walked through the door carrying some beautifully wrapped gifts. Pickle smiled watching as Sidney beamed at Mrs Wonders. A tiny little 'POP!' she chuckled, Mrs Wonders had been alone far too long. "Gifts?" Queried Mummy. "yes gifts kind of, but to keep you all safe, no more not knowing where everyone is." Mrs Wonders passed them around. One for everyone, even Pickle and Sidney, some for him to take home to his friends, and lastly two for Mr and Mrs Wormchuck. Opening the parcels, they were delighted to find exact copies of bangles, all differing in size. Each were given the instructions to wear it at all times. "Now we call them Bangles because when you are in need you BANG your bangle on whatever it is you have next to you or even on your leg. "Sidney would you like to demonstrate please?" Only too delighted to help Mrs Wonders he immediately BANGED his wrist down on the table. A lightning bolt fell from the sky, a magnificent green and gold colour, it stopped just above the bangle on Sidney's wrist. Wherever he moved his wrist, the lightening bolt followed. He couldn't shake it off, no matter how he tried. He began to smile, "very clever," was his response. "So you see, if we can't see you and you are in trouble, this happens, it'll point to directly to where you are, you must never take it off, any of you."

Daddy and Marmalade decided to fill the dishwasher together, they had already asked if he would like to attend the party, he had agreed it would be a wonderful thing to do so, plus he could show everyone how clever he was at washing up at the same time.

Marmalade looked at Daddy. "I was yours once wasn't I?" "Yes Marmalade, yes you were. It was a long time ago. I am more than happy that you are with us now and that you are looking after Ebony and keeping her safe, thank you my dear dear friend." Marmalade blushed. "I will always look after her, no matter what."

Chapter 18

The Party.

Sidney called his friends back up from the depths. They were enjoying food and drink they had never seen or tasted before. Talking with all the others they had wonderful if not scary stories to tell and heard exciting stories back in return.

One by one more and more guests arrived. Mrs Wonders was busy making her Punchypunchfruityfuit Drink, everyone claimed it was the loveliest drink that ever they had tasted but of course with it being Mrs Wonders who had made it, it was bound to have something special added, making it taste of something completely delicious and different to each person.

Cheerypops was in his element, he was wearing a Chef's Hat for this very special occasion, smiling and whistling as he baked, he was baking a strawberry and cream gateaux, having already made sausage rolls, egg and cress sandwiches, quiches of every flavour and breads of every design. Mummy had placed large plates of cheeses and cold meats all over the tables, bunches of grapes decorated the platters. Fruit of every description overfilled bowls. Chocolates were floating in bowls around the marquee offering themselves to the guests. Sally octopus stayed near her pool at all times she was scared of drying out, Mrs Wonders told her it was perfectly safe for her to come out and talk with the others, delighted she offered everyone a merry-go-round ride. Music was playing and the pirates started singing their sea shanties of days gone by. Everyone was having a wonderful time.

"Pickle, where are all the other fairies?" Ebony asked her. Pickle giggled. "Remember your cake? Well," pointing to an enormous extraordinary orange cat cake exactly the same as the one from Ebony's party, which was now flying it's way over to a table in the marquee. "you can never have enough cake can you? Cheerypops remembered the recipe and baked us another one, there was enough left of the extraordinary orange cat cake colour to make an exact replica. Mummy looked at Mrs Wonders. "Two of them?" Mrs Wonders mouth dropped open, was this a good idea?

The cake was finally in place, Ebony and Marmalade went over to look. "For you all to enjoy, another Marmalade cake." The fairies flicked their wands and stars landed on and slipped into the cake.

The cake stood up, stretched and... "Hello everyone, my name is Paws, how lovely to meet you all, you can call me Dashing, because I am rather, aren't I?"

Marmalade gasped... "oh brother!"

Everyone laughed, this was definately going to be the start of something strange. Again.

THE END

A Little About The Author.

Hello, my name is Alison Jarvis, I am an author, writing poetry and short stories for adults as well as a new venture into children's stories.

Ebony is the first book in a planned series of stories. Each book will introduce new characters and will see the start of a new adventure.

I live in Oxfordshire with my family.

Thank you to my family and to my friends and thank you for reading my book, I hope you have enjoyed it.

Stay safe.

Printed in Poland
by Amazon Fulfillment
Poland Sp. z o.o., Wrocław